# KISMET

# KISMET

---

Alie Day

Tamarind Hill Press

www.tamarindhillpress.co.uk

First published in 2019

London, United Kingdom



ISBN

978-1-64570-000-0

**TAMARiND HiLL**
**.PRESS**

# DEDICATION

*For Nanny Hazel, who believed in my scribblings before anyone else.*

# ACKNOWLEDGEMENTS

Seeing Kismet published is something I have dreamed of since pen hit paper. I hope you all love Nick, Sasha and the rest of the gang as much as I do.

This book wouldn't exist if it wasn't for the support of my loving family and my amazing friends and editor.

My soul mate, Jack - you keep me sane, drive me crazy and support me through everything all in the same breath. I would not have had the courage to revisit this book or start writing again without your love and support. I am so lucky to be able to share my life and all of my terrible jokes with you. Thank you for everything you do, everything you are and for being the person I get to come home to at the end of the day.

Tamarind Hill Press - Thank you for believing in Kismet and what it could become. You made this book possible, and for that, I am forever grateful.

# Table of Contents

# CHAPTER ONE
*Nick*

Jenna Green was everything I'd ever wanted or so I'd thought. Jenna was kind, beautiful, always smiling, blonde, smart and she was safe. Maybe that was the problem.

Jenna and I had been together for three years and maybe that was why I was so blind to the gallon of crazy that lurked behind her emerald eyes. We'd met at university after being introduced by my best friend CJ and we had instantly gotten along. I'd be lying if I said I didn't find her attractive straight away but it took us five excruciatingly long years to finally get our shit together and make ourselves a couple. In those five years, I'd had several hook-ups and a couple of girlfriends but nothing really stuck. When I eventually figured out it was Jenna who I wanted, everything just seemed to work out; at least until the night everything seemed to change.

*

Jenna had been staying at my flat for around two weeks. Her parents were renovating and she didn't exactly want to spend all her time in a hotel with them. They were not the easiest people to get along with. Anyway, she'd been staying a while and one night we were about to order dinner, and she just came out with it; "I think I should move in here." At first, I thought she was joking. I mean, really, who just invites themselves to live in someone else's home without even the slightest discussion first? But when I stopped laughing nervously, I noticed that the corners of her mouth had turned down and her cheeks had turned an alarming shade of red. I cleared my throat and prepared myself for a slap. What I was about to say would surely earn me one.

"What makes you think that?" I asked, dragging the words out nervously.

Her eyebrows knitted together at an altogether too sharp angle, and her fingers clutched at her knees aggressively, causing her sharp nails to leave half-moon shaped dents in her skin. Jenna had always said she didn't like conflict, but that didn't mean a few fits of rage weren't stored up in her slender body.

"What the hell is that supposed to mean?" she hissed.

"Well, I don't know. I just kind of feel like you just invited yourself to live in my home." I didn't want to argue but she knows how important this place is to me.

"It's not like you didn't see it coming, I've been living here for two weeks!"

"Just because you've been staying here, doesn't mean I expected you to want to move in. Jeez, what's next, marriage and kids?" Okay, that one was kind of harsh.

"God, Nick. All I wanted was to bring us a little closer together. No need to be a total asshole about it." She stood up, picking her plate up from the coffee table and taking it into the kitchen without another word. I had to follow her of course because I'd only be in more trouble if I didn't. I just wish I could make her see things my way.

"Look, I'm sorry. You just caught me by surprise, okay?" I said under my breath, kissing her neck softly as she scrubbed at her plate furiously.

"You don't get to just kiss me and think I'm going to melt into your arms and surrender. It doesn't work like that," she huffed, squirming away from me.

"I just thought I'd apologise. I was out of order but you did catch me by surprise."

"Why don't you want me to move in?" she asked, turning to face me with hurt and confusion all over her face. I wanted to be able to explain it in a way she'd understand but I knew deep down that she just wouldn't get it.

"It's not that I don't want you to move in but you need to understand that this flat was my turning point: getting away from that life and from everything. It all started here and inviting someone else into it with the intention of living here, now that is a really weird thought for me," I admitted, being entirely truthful.

"So what? Are you going to live here forever, a bachelor at heart, telling your long-term girlfriends that they're not welcome just because you had a sucky childhood?"

That was all it needed; one comment about my childhood, and then I saw red. "Get out," I said, breathing deeply through my nose. In that moment I couldn't think about anything but getting her out of my house before the flashbacks of my childhood ensued. She knew better than to bring it up like that but she did it anyway, with that same callous disregard for the emotions of others; I'd seen it in her so many times before.

"Excuse me?" she said sharply, her voice pitching up with the anger boiling just under the surface.

"Get. Out. Pack up your stuff and *leave*. We're done," I told her, leaving the kitchen and heading straight for my office.

I locked the door and dropped down into the expensive, leather office chair that sat wedged in the corner. I'd saved for far too long for this chair and it was already showing signs of great use. Its twin sat in my room at work. I turned on my laptop and then looked at my phone, thinking about the past and waiting for Jenna to get the hell out of my home. She'd had no right to bring up my past. She had no right to go there, no matter how upset she'd been with me.

I was still fuming when Jenna eventually knocked on the door. "Nick, are you still in there?" she asked.

"Yes," I called, sighing with agitation. "Are you leaving now?"

"Don't be silly, I know you didn't mean it. I've just been out to get some air and to think a little. I know what I said was out of order and I'm sorry." Her tone was almost patronising, like she thought I wouldn't stand my ground.

I shook my head. I could imagine her face: mouth turning down, cheeks flushing and eyes full of remorse. However, all my mind registered was that she'd ignored my request for her to leave. "I asked you to leave Jenna. I asked you to pack your bags and get out, so why are you still here? Did you think I was joking? Did you think I was having a laugh?" I said through the door, teeth gritted in frustration.

"It's really hard to talk to you with this lump of wood in my face. Would you just let me in?"

"Why should I? You'll only set up camp and never leave." The venom in my voice surprised even me but I was standing my ground. I had to.

"You don't really want me to leave, do you? You're not serious Nick." She sounded worried, but I didn't feel bad. I just really wanted her to get out.

I threw open the door and looked her straight in the eye. "I need you to get out Jenna. I need you to leave and I need you not to contact me until I contact you. Please." I glared, and eventually she sighed and walked down the hall into my bedroom. I heard a bag opening and I felt relieved. I shut the door again but I didn't bother locking it. I knew she wouldn't come in now.

Jenna left about two hours after the final argument. She left a letter taped to the front door but I didn't read it. I would later, but right then I just didn't want to. You might be thinking, 'this is so weird, why is he just throwing her out after a little spat?' Well, the truth is, I'd been dodging arguments with Jenna for months. She kept trying to push me to do things and there's only so much a person can take. Jenna and I had been falling apart at the seams for far too long and although I loved her, I couldn't take much more. Her dismissal of the seriousness of my past had been the final straw. I'd always noticed how she dodged the subject or brushed it off whenever I could muster up the courage to talk about it. I hadn't realised until tonight how dismissive she was of my past though. I hadn't noticed how dismissive she was of my emotions.

I phoned Jenna two days later to tell her it was over. She asked me why and I told her I felt we'd grown apart. She cried and I asked her not to. She told me I was a dick but I stayed quiet and eventually all that was left was relief - for me anyway. I'd loved Jenna with all my heart but I was beginning to feel ill every time I was with her. My palms would sweat; I'd feel sick and that bad, anxiety-filled version of butterflies that I always used to get before exams would rise aggressively in my stomach. Deep down, I knew it was because we were both wasting our time. I knew it was because we just weren't right for each other.

A week after the breakup, my best friend CJ showed up at the flat after I'd pretty much ignored every text, tweet and inbox, totally keeping to myself through fear of having to 'talk about it'. The summer was almost over but I had no enthusiasm for the sunshine and I was looking forward to getting back to work. CJ didn't think that was the right way of thinking. He barged through my front door dressed way too smartly to just be 'popping over' and after twenty long minutes of him trying to act casual, jumping from foot to foot and talking nonstop, I finally asked why he was really here.

"There is this awesome band playing at Fivers tonight and you, my friend, are coming," he said, seriously.

Fivers was a shoddy music club about ten minutes away from my flat. We'd been going there since our first year of university because it was literally only a fiver to get in all year round, except Christmas Eve, when it was free. It didn't matter what bands were playing, you got tickets for a fiver and that was that. The drinks at Fivers were the cheapest in town and it had an all-around great atmosphere, but tonight, I did not fancy Fivers. "CJ, mate, I'm really not up for it tonight," I groaned, sitting on the arm of my worn, black leather sofa from some charity shop my grandmother had passed by when I was just moving in.

"Yes, you *are*. You love Fivers, and you need to get out before you turn into a grey and boring old man. You're already half way there anyway; I'll be buying you a Zimmer frame for your birthday if you're not careful." He grinned and headed to the kitchen. "Get ready, I'll grab you a beer," he called authoritatively.

I shook my head, admitting defeat and went to my bedroom to change. I pulled on some black jeans and a semi smart shirt. Jenna had never liked me wearing shirts and tonight was going to be the first night that I didn't have to take that into consideration. Okay, I didn't actually think of that until after I'd put the shirt on but still. I wandered into the kitchen and opened the beer CJ had left on the counter. "So, what bands are playing tonight?" I asked. He mentioned some names I didn't recognise and played me a couple of songs on his phone. By the time we'd finished discussing which songs we liked best, we'd finished our beers and it was time to leave.

Fivers looked like it had cost a fiver inside and out. It was shabby and old, and looked like it had been furnished by an old man who smoked a pipe and wore a flat cap. CJ and I had loved the place from the moment we'd set foot in it and had spent the majority of our years at university there too. It stank of stale beer and sweat. The smell of old cigarette smoke from before smoking was banned still clung to every wall and surface, but it was definitely the place to be. Maybe it was the old stories embedded in the minds of the owners and the grains in the wooden floors or maybe it was the atmosphere that the ghosts of gigmas past gave off or the totally down to earth people you met there. Who knows? Whatever it was, the place was addicting and probably one of the very few reasons that we'd never moved out of Ravens End. It had taken us ten minutes to get here and we'd used the longer route. Luckily for us, the queue had barely started to form, so we knew we would get a good spot when we went in.

I'd been staring into space for a while, when behind me, I heard a melodic voice talking quietly to much more excitable voices. I turned, casually, feigning looking at the length of the queue and discovered that the wonderful voice belonged to an incredibly enchanting girl. She had dark, loosely curly hair that tumbled over her shoulders and spilled down her back. She was wearing dark blue, ripped skinny jeans and what looked like grubby white converse, with a tight vest top that had a fierce looking tiger on the front. She was petite but curvy in the right areas and her top definitely proved that she knew that. She caught me staring and looked up at me with big, gorgeous blue eyes, thickly framed with dark lashes and dark eye makeup. Her mouth curved into a beautifully flirtatious smile that almost looked unintentional. For the few seconds that we locked eyes, I was totally under her spell. When the queue started to move, life seemed to fast forward and I was left with an irritating nagging sensation on my mind.

"Who was that delicious chick?" CJ asked, his face too close to my ear as we were pushed and shoved as less polite people tried to get into the club. He eyed the enchantress as she slipped by us to get to the front of the now thickening crowd in front of the stage.

"I don't know mate but hands off," I muttered, slapping him on the back before weaving my way through the sea of people to keep my eye on her from a distance. CJ followed me in and tried to scope the crowd for a girl of his own to hook up with. He eventually found one and vowed to look for her after the show.

The show was pretty incredible and all of the bands had definitely earned themselves a spot on my iTunes and CD rack. However, after the initial merch buys and quick drinks at the bar, I was way too eager to look for the enchantress to think of much else. After what felt like hours of searching, I finally spotted her leaning against a wall next to the stage. There were maybe three or four girls standing around her, all talking at once while she listened. She seemed to be taking in every word each person said, and when they finally stopped jabbering, she replied to each of them in turn, looking at each of them adoringly as if she were a parent. There was clearly something special about this girl, and there was an ache sliding around under my skin that said I needed to speak to her, hear her voice, and feel her skin brush against mine.

I waded through the still milling crowd, feeling the heat of the colourful lights and mingling bodies against my skin as I locked eyes once again with the enchanting girl. Her intense stare pulled me forward until my live wired body was only inches from hers. "Want to dance?" I asked, feeling relieved when she pushed away from the wall she was propping up and grabbed my hand. Her touch sent slivers of electricity through my veins as she dragged me into the ocean of tightly compacted bodies. I put my hands on her waist as she threw her hands above her head and let the music take her. Our bodies moulded together as we moved as one, feeling the vibrations of the pulsing beat shake through our bones in a dizzy cluster of moments that would flash through my mind and dreams for weeks to come. I watched her with hungry eyes as she bit her lip, looking up at me in the final moments of the last song, and that was the selling point. That one, tiny gesture was all I needed to close the minuscule amount of distance between us and press my lips urgently to hers. I could taste the salt of sweat and felt the eagerness of her mind as our two worlds collided. Her hands moved from my chest to my neck almost as urgently as mine went from her waist to her hair. We were lost in a perfect moment of racing pulses, lips, tongues and teeth grazing lips when a cough told us we should probably cool it. We pulled away, smiling sheepishly at each other with our fingers linking, clearly not quite believing what we'd just done, before stepping away and now at a loss as to where to go from here. "Nick Lacey," I introduced, smiling with genuine happiness for the first time in a long time.

"Sasha Santiago," she replied, blushing and looking around distractedly when her friend called her, giggling. "I guess I'll see you around," she smiled, kissing me lightly on the cheek before disappearing into the dead of night, leaving me with just the memory of her lips against mine.

"Woah man," CJ breathed, clapping his hand on my shoulder as we walked out of the bar.

I woke up the next morning feeling alive. It took me a few seconds to remember why and when I did, I felt so guilty but it was the happiest I'd been in a long while at the same time. Last night had been the first time in months that I had felt such a strong connection and appeal to another person. Jenna and I had lost our spark somewhere towards the end of our relationship but I guess before last night, I'd not even noticed.

My phone was still in my jeans and after I plugged it in to charge, I noticed I had a couple of Facebook notifications. The first was a friend request from Sasha and it said she'd requested two hours ago, which meant she'd waited until she'd woken up to friend me. I accepted a little too quickly and checked my other notification; an inbox from Jenna's sister, Sara.

"Nick, I know you and Jenna have had problems recently and everything but it's been a week now. Don't you think it's time to end this game and get back together?"

I sighed at the message, shaking my head. Trust Jenna to get her sister involved. Sara was usually an influential and extremely persuasive woman, but today she was just a sibling sticking her nose in, and I was *not* going to just get back with Jenna because Sara told me to.

"I'm only going to say this once; Jenna and I are done. We've been trying to make it work for months and it's just not happening. You can tell her I'm sorry, but deep down she knows this was destined to end long ago."

I was about to leave my phone on the side and walk away when another message came through. It was Sasha.

"Hey, :)"

# CHAPTER TWO

*Sasha*

*Two years ago*

My palms were sweaty and I was completely freaking out. The brightly lit photo on the phone in front of me was all the proof I needed to tell me that I'd been right all along. Jase had been cheating, and he'd been cheating for a long time. He had text me to say he'd be late coming over tonight and until today, I'd only ever been suspicious. Now that I'd seen proof of his skeevy little meetings, I was almost sure he'd been with one of his sluts just today. I sighed deeply to myself. I had liked Jase so much for such a long time and I had convinced myself I was falling for him, but things had felt wrong since day one and I was starting to wonder if I had made the biggest mistake. Deep down, I think I'd known it all along.

Jase and I had been friends for years and I'd had a crush on him for most of that time. I guess somewhere along the line he decided he liked me too, because one day, out of the blue, he asked me out on a date. I was so overly excited about it that I didn't even register how out of the blue it was. I personally thought our date was amazing but the day after, he texted me and told me he didn't think dating was the way for us to go. A few hours later, he had a new girlfriend and I was falling apart at the seams. It had taken me months to get over Jase and his tricks. I'd thought he was so perfect with his short, dark hair and strangely beautiful eyes; I could never really figure out their true colour. He was a bad boy or so he made himself out to be and I couldn't help but think that maybe I was too much of a good girl for him. None of my friends knew Jase. They had seen pictures and they thought he was attractive but it stopped there. He was a year older and went to a different school, so my two lives were separate, but for some reason, he seemed to just know what I was like at school. He somehow knew that I was less brave, quieter and normally ended up eating lunch in the loo by myself.

We hadn't spoken since the day he told me things wouldn't work out, but almost four months later, he was waiting for me outside the school gates with my favourite flavour ice cream in a cone in his hand and a lopsided, goofy looking grin on his face. I wanted to be angry, to ignore him and leave, but that smile and those eyes; they drew me in and I was lost. He told me he'd broken up with his girlfriend and that he'd seen the light, realised he liked me and asked if I'd give him another chance. I was a fool to say yes, and I'd been a fool for three and a half months since. Tonight was the night things had to change and suddenly, after all the worrying and fretting, I heard a knock at the door. I felt strong and real, ready to face whatever ugliness was about to try to break me.

Jase stepped into my house and grinned, leaning in to hug me. I didn't hug him back and he pulled away, confused. "What's up?" he asked, shrugging off his hoodie to reveal a t-shirt I'd bought him for his birthday. I rolled my eyes and stood by the sofa.

"There's no easy way to say this Jase but I think we should break up," I said coldly.

"What?" He blinked at me, trying his best to look like a puppy. I didn't fall for it.

"I know what you've been up to and to be honest, I'm just not interested anymore. I'd really appreciate it if you could take your things on the way out. They're by the door." I watched his eyes follow my gaze to the box by the front door, feeling a strange sense of relief and satisfaction when he huffed and kicked the box a little before he left.

After Jase and I broke up, I'd found out that he'd been cheating with not only one girl but five and that they had all known about me. That was hard to hear, but what was harder was the sound of his car outside my house every night and the feeling of being watched everywhere I went.

Finally, my parents got sick of the stalking and called the police. However, when they wouldn't do anything, the 'rents decided it was time to pack up and leave, and that's when we headed to Ravens End. It was an easy decision, easier than deciding what to wear on a non-uniform day. I didn't have much to leave behind, since leaving school meant that my old friends and I had drifted apart and my college friends were the kind of people that wouldn't bother staying in touch. I was excited to get out and do something new. Who doesn't want to see what a new life would be like at seventeen?

Ravens End did take a while to get used to. It was a level of stepford that even the most imaginative minds couldn't comprehend, but once you learned not to create scandal or at least how to hide it if you did, it was actually a pretty charming place. The streets were always immaculate, the birds sang beautifully and every season brought a new, deliciously 'at home' feeling when it arrived. There wasn't much to do in Ravens End but somehow, it didn't matter. We managed to make our own fun, and hiding or uncovering scandals was one of most people's favourite habits, so having fun on the down low actually became half the fun of having fun in the first place. I made friends easily and it wasn't too hard to catch up with my work, considering classes had only been going for a couple of months. Everything was hunky-dory, completely un-scandalous and fabulously fine for an entire year, and I guess that brings us to the now...

*Present Day:*

I hadn't had a relationship in two years. Jase was my last boyfriend and I was really starting to notice my lack of romance. What was worse? So were my friends. I hadn't had secret hook ups like they had and I hadn't been lusting over every guy that looked my way. I'd taken up the position of the aunt of our little group, listening, giving advice, keeping everyone sane, and I'd stay that way as long as my friends needed me to. However, they were really starting to notice my lack of a man to double date with, and they were starting to scold me for turning people down. I was pretty sure they had all sorts of theories as to what was wrong with me, but the truth was I just didn't want another bad relationship. I wanted and needed to be happy and getting into a bad relationship was not going to make that happen. It sounded cliché and girly, but I just wanted to find someone to settle down with instead of having to deal with the dirty shame of one one-night-stand after the other.

My best friend Kate was lying on my bed, giggling manically at her phone. "What's your problem?" I asked, turning away from my computer to see her blushing and grinning.

"Sid wants to meet up tonight and he's got this whole plan of things he wants to do." She waggled her eyebrows and sighed.

"You told him you're still a virgin didn't you?" I shook my head with mock disapproval.

"Yep!" She grinned predictably and sat up, still glued to her phone.

"How many more guys are you going to say that to? They're going to catch on sooner or later; there's not much left of Ravens End you haven't slept with," I scolded.

"That's so not true! I stick within a three year age gap, don't I?"

"Yes and when you've run out, what will you do? Terrorise some toy boys or go for the pensioners?" I teased.

She threw a pillow at me and poked her tongue out. "Alright miss perfect, at least I'm not completely celibate like you." She grinned again and I glared at her.

"I'm not celibate; I'm just not willing to sleep with any randomer that crosses my path. What is your problem with that lately?" I asked.

"People are starting to think you have some kind of secret and you know what secrets do to the people in this place. I'm trying to protect you, not hurt you," she said quietly.

"Yeah, I know. I just don't want to be with someone for the sake of it or for the idea of being in a relationship. I want it to be right, not a whole bunch of fake."

"I get you, I do and I know we don't live our lives the same way but I wish you'd come out with me and the girls just once; you might enjoy it. I know you like that Fivers place, so why don't we go there as a group? We'll get dressed up, have some fun and you can at least scope out some guys." She smiled, actually looking away from her phone for once. I got the impression that she really didn't 'get me' as she'd said. It was one thing to be looking out for a friend but a completely different kettle of fish trying to force your friend into hooking up with someone.

"Fine, but I'm not hooking up with anyone okay?" I sighed, knowing full well I wouldn't be able to change her mind.

"Okay," she agreed, looking at the time on my alarm clock, "Shit, I have to go. Discuss deets later?" she asked. I nodded, and watched her leave, turning back to my computer and typing out the last few sentences of the article I was writing on a really great band for a magazine.

By the time Kate phoned me about details, I was already freaking out. Why had I agreed to this? I'd started going to Fivers after my 18th birthday and I only ever went on my own when good bands were playing. I'd never taken friends there and I knew they wouldn't be too pleased with the appearance of the place. They may not enjoy the stepford qualities of the town, but they didn't want to be tarred with the same brush as some of the riffraff that hung out at Fivers. Some people who went to Fivers were dead classy but they'd be so discreet about it that no one else would ever know. I usually kept to myself there, wearing jeans and hoodies and keeping myself on the down low, just because I preferred not to interact with most people. This time though we were supposed to be getting dolled up, looking glamorous and ready to take on the entire crowd. I was so not equipped for that and Kate knew it.

When the day of the Fivers trip finally came around, I was still no closer to deciding what to wear, how to do my makeup or what to do with my hair. The hours were ticking by rapidly and I had to come up with something before Kate did it for me and if she did it for me, I'd look like a demented marshmallow.

I finally settled on some extremely comfortable ripped skinny jeans and a newly acquired tight vest top with a beautiful picture of a roaring tiger on it. It had spaghetti straps and rhinestones around the eyes, and it was perfectly me. It also made my boobs look amazing. I went with dark, semi gothic looking eyes and my favourite blood red lip stain. I put strawberry lip gloss over the top and pulled on my ever-faithful white converse. I let my hair dry in its natural loose, curly waves and sprayed the hell out of it before I set off to pick up Kate. Being the only non-drinker of the group, I was picked as the designated driver. Par for the course really.

We managed to fit six of us very illegally into my car, with our friend Penelope lying on the floor in the back. It was probably more illegal than drunk driving but Fivers wasn't a long way away and we figured collectively that it would be okay for just one trip. I parked up out back, knowing it was free to anyone visiting and lead the way to the queue at the front of the venue. The girls huddled around me, gossiping about bitches and giggling about guys. I took my usual position as the advice giver and voice of reason, taking in segments of each conversation so that I could keep everyone happy. This had been my life for just over a year and I was so good at it by now that I barely even needed both ears to listen. I was stopped midway through a sentence by a pair of deliciously warm, dark brown eyes staring at me. I let my eyes adjust so that they could focus on the face the eyes belonged to and saw something equally warm in the smile of a stranger. He had shortish dark brown, wavy hair, and a wide, kind looking smile. His lips looked entirely too kissable with their slight disproportion like the angular cupids bow and I was taken by surprise by the pins and needles making my entire body ache longingly at the sight of him. He was wearing a button down casual shirt and jeans. I know rationally he looked like a regular guy but to me, he looked like a god.

I wasn't sure if I was feeling this way because of what Kate had said about people talking about me, so I squashed down the need to separate the crowd and press my lips against his and settled for smiling shyly at him. Out of nowhere, the queue started to move and I was too busy trying to make sure that all my friends were okay to think about the delicious guy. However, my insides still felt like melted chocolate from the brief encounter.

When we were inside, we all linked arms as I snaked us through the crowd to the front. After the initial shock of being sandwiched between random strangers like rigid sardines in a tin, my friends started to look like they were actually enjoying themselves, which meant I could finally relax and enjoy the music. I liked two of the bands out of three, which wasn't bad. I wasn't an easy critic and I knew that was one of my many flaws but I just didn't enjoy listening to the second band's set. I'd probably give them a second chance if I found them online, but I couldn't make promises. I'm nothing if not honest. Not that I went up to the band and told them I wasn't keen or anything, I just didn't rush over to buy all of their merch.

After the show ended, I found a nice spot near the stage to stand; a perfect little gap where I could lean against the wall. I didn't expect my friends to huddle round me for Aunt Sasha time but apparently, they needed to. I followed the regular procedure, listening to as much of each situation as necessary and answering each of them with my advice in turn. After I was done, I looked up to see Mr. Delicious walking towards me. "Want to dance?" he asked with a Ravens End accent in his deep voice.

Every single nerve in my body felt like it was on fire and all I wanted to do was feel his arms around me and his body against mine. So I pushed away from the wall and dragged him into the undulating crowd. I hoped he wouldn't mind being in the middle of a ton or more happy couples grinding against each other desperately under the lights. When we found a relatively comfortable space, he put his hands on my waist and I let the thumping pulse of the beat drive me. With our bodies pushed closely together, I was aware of how electric this guy was making me feel and I was feeling more and more attracted to him by the second. It was like meeting this random stranger had unleashed something inside me that I didn't even know was there before. I don't know how long we danced for, but every moment was filled with heated sparks and flickers of fire that danced along my skin whenever our bodies were in contact.

Eventually, the music ended and I was highly aware of how sweaty we both were but somehow I didn't care. There was a split second between our eyes interlocking and me making the decision to kiss him, and that second was so charged that it was almost unbearable. I pressed my lips to his and let my fingers flutter over his chest and up to his neck, before resting there to play gently with the short hair at the nape of his neck. His tongue slid into my mouth, exploring it like Indiana Jones on an expedition. I hadn't been kissed like this probably ever, and it was the most exhilarating, most beautiful experience I'd ever come across. I let him dominate the kiss completely until eventually, it was time to pull away. I suddenly felt self-conscious and shy. What if I'd been a bad kisser and he regretted it? I smiled nervously at him and saw a glint in his eye that made me feel calmer again. I was relieved when he entwined his fingers with mine. Out of nowhere, I was snapped out of my reverie by Kate calling out to me, giggling like she knew exactly what was going on in my mind and letting me know that was my cue to leave.

"Nick Lacey," he smiled, introducing himself. Even his name caused goose bumps to prickle at the surface of my skin.

"Sasha Santiago," I replied, smiling before I turned to meet my friends.

After I made sure everyone was home safely, I could finally get myself home. Kate had been bugging me all the way to hers about the kiss with the stranger, Nick, but I wasn't telling. I didn't want my perfect moment to be ruined by a drunken dissection after all.

When I was lying in my bed, staring at the ceiling, I replayed the moment in my head over and over and over, trying to find fault but not coming up with any. I searched his name on Facebook and was gutted when his profile was completely private. His picture was too small for me to make out his face properly, but I decided I'd probably add him in the morning. I fell asleep to the memory of his lips and his voice and eventually resurfaced at around ten am. I turned on my phone straight away and creeped my twitter feed for around ten minutes before opening up Facebook. I typed in Nick's name quickly and pressed the 'send friend request' button with my thumb, feeling nervous for the next two hours while I waited to see if he'd accept. When he eventually did, I suddenly became wildly adventurous and messaged him a simple message, spending a little too long trying to decide whether to add an 'x' or not. I decided to try to be casual and went with no.

"Hey, :)." I wrote, feeling my heart thump as I waited for a reply.

# CHAPTER THREE
*Nick*

I took a few minutes to reply. I wanted to seem casual but those few minutes felt like hours.

"Hey x," I replied.

"So, last night was, uh, weird." I felt a lump form in my throat, had she hated it?

"I guess," I responded, my palms feeling sweaty at the thought of losing whatever hope had risen up within me last night.

"I mean weird good. Sorry, I've never kissed a stranger in a club before." Relief washed over me as I reached behind me to check my bed was within sitting proximity, not taking my eyes off the screen for even a second.

"Good to hear ;)."

"Haha, how about you though, was I just one of your many or?" I laughed. She had to be joking, right? It's not like I look like the kind of guy that plays around.

"No, I was taken, until recently," I admitted.

"Ah, so I was a rebound?"

"No, nothing about that kiss was a rebound."

"Good to hear ;)."

"My turn, how about you though? What made you kiss a stranger in a club?"

"Now if I told you that, I'd have to kill you ;). Actually, speaking of killing people, my best friend wants to hear about my stranger kissing antics, so I'll speak to you later? :) x."

"Sure and make sure you tell her how great I am ;) x," I replied, smiling to myself and feeling as warm and fuzzy as a care bear. She was funny and I liked that. I knew so little about her, yet she was already so far from the type of person Jenna was and for the first time in months, I was actually smiling.

I showered and got dressed, feeling better than I had for a while, and decided to see if CJ wanted to do something. To get him back for barging into my flat yesterday, I decided to climb through his front window and make a fuck ton of noise so he'd think he was being burgled. Unfortunately for me, CJ was already in his living room, so my plan failed. I silently vowed to get him back soon though. I sat on his windowsill and waited for whatever was about to come out of CJ's extremely unpredictable mouth. "Dude," he grinned, "didn't take you long, did it? Should I call you 'Captain Nick' now? Would you like a drink your majesty?"

I sighed at his childish ways. "I'll take a coffee if you're offering and well, 'Captain Nick' does have a ring to it," I joked as I followed him into the kitchen and sat on a bar stool while he boiled the kettle.

"Too bad you didn't get her number man, she could've been a great little rebound."

"If my sister was here right now, she'd be calling you a pig." I shook my head, catching the change in CJ's expression when I mentioned Cat. "Anyway, who needs numbers when you have Facebook?"

"You've already added her? Talk about desperate mate. And speaking of Cat, how is she?" he asked, trying not to give away the depth of his interest. Ever since he'd met my sister four years ago, CJ had been dealing with the most girly crush I'd ever seen him have. CJ was all about being a lad but when it came to Cat, he had a weak spot that even heavy armour couldn't protect. It may have something to do with the fact that my sister is some kind of fashion model with the personality of a mad scientist or it may just be CJ being weirdly obsessed with a girl that looks a little like his best mate. Who knows? But either way, it made him jumpy and freakishly girl-like.

"She's good. I think she did some catwalk thing in Paris a few weeks ago. She met some actor dude called Paulo Yvonne, and they seem to be hitting it off. Would you like me to mention you asked after her?" I teased.

"Don't be a dick. Is she still living with your mother or what?" I winced at the mention of my mother, feeling the familiar rolling sickness of anxiety fill up my stomach.

"I think Cat is still in Paris or at least she was last I heard. I haven't spoken to my mother, so I wouldn't know for sure." I wasn't in the mood for talking about this. "Actually, I heard from Cat that Dad went to see her in Paris and offered to let her live with him if she wanted. I told her I think she should take the opportunity to get away from mum, but I don't know if she'll listen." I sighed. "Back to last night though, did you end up meeting anyone?" I asked.

"Nah mate, got chatting to one of the bands and lost track of time. I think you had enough fun for the both of us though, right?"

"She was perfect and enchanting. I don't know how to describe it but I felt like I was drawn to her."

"Aw, did she cast a little spell on you?" he teased, making me flip him off.

"Laugh all you want, but this is no better than that time you wore that entirely salmon pink coloured suit to try to impress Cat."

"That was a mistake and I was misled, by you, might I add. So what kind of girl is this chick then?" I must have looked at him with a confused expression because he quickly elaborated. "You haven't snooped around her Facebook, have you?" I shook my head. "Let me grab my laptop."

After snooping around her Facebook page for an hour, CJ had come to a conclusion. He had decided that Sasha was 'definitely a smoking hot chick, and not secretly a man.' She wasn't a slut but she wasn't afraid to flaunt her assets and she was popular but didn't really seem to care. She was tagged in thousands of photos and there were tons of posts on her wall, but her replies all seemed lacking. Eventually, we discovered her twitter account and realised she was much more of a tweeter. In fact, '@SashaSant' had tweeted just over 43,000 times in total but disappointingly, only four times since last night, all about how she wished '@KateSparklele' would get out of her house. The fifth tweet down her timeline was much more promising. She'd put a smiley face probably about five minutes after she left Fivers. I smiled to myself and followed her, wondering if she'd realise it was me.

I left CJ's at about six and headed home. We had played video games for most of the day, enjoying our last, true day of freedom as CJ liked to call it. We'd be back to work in three days and the next two would be spent planning lessons and wondering why we'd decided lecturing at the college could ever be a good idea. It struck me as funny how CJ could be the most immature person in the world but was also the best teacher I knew.

I had an unpleasant surprise sitting on my doorstep when I got home in the form of Jenna. "What do you want?" I asked, stepping around her to open my door. That was a mistake. I should have shooed her off before she'd have a chance at getting inside. She stood up and asked to come in. I told her I wasn't sure it was a good idea, but she pushed past me anyway. "Well, I'm getting changed; you can wait for me in the living room," I muttered, heading up the hallway to change into a different t-shirt. I didn't need to change at all, but I needed a moment to compose myself. My phone made the Facebook messenger dinging sound and smiled when I saw who it was: Sasha.

'So, my friend is finally done quizzing me. How hard is it to dig a shallow grave in the woods?' She asked. I laughed to myself.

'Not that hard, it gets easier the more you do it.'

'Nice. How's your day been?'

'Good up until now. The ex was on my doorstep when I got home. I've been hiding in my room for the past five minutes pretending to change.' I pulled my t-shirt over my head and threw on a fresh one.

I just needed a moment to compose myself. Jenna's presence was still making me angry, despite her stupid comments being long forgotten about by her.

'Bravery is overrated right?' I was glad Sasha didn't ask any other questions.

';) I should probably find out what she wants.'

'Sure thing. Talk later :).' This girl was so easy to talk to. I was impressed by the fact that she didn't bat an eyelid at the fact that my ex is in my flat. Maybe she's make believe. I put my phone back into my pocket and went back down the hall to the living room. Jenna was sitting neatly on the arm chair that used to be hers, looking as comfortable as ever and making me completely uneasy. I perched on the arm of my sofa, trying to make sure there was as little familiarity in the situation as possible.

"What do you want, Jenna?" I asked, watching her eyes roam the room as she swept her shiny blonde hair up into a clip.

"This is getting stupid now Nick. When are you going to man up and apologise for kicking me out? I know we can work this out, we're soulmates," she cried, sounding urgent, dragging out the last word as if it added more weight to her point. It didn't.

"Okay firstly, what do I have to apologise for? You treat me like some joke and act as if I'm your pet project: the guy that whines because he 'had a sucky childhood', and you invite yourself to live with me, with no warning and no hints from me that I want you to do so. Secondly, Jen, there was a time I thought we were destined for each other but I don't see it that way anymore. If you're honest with yourself, you'll notice that things hadn't been right for a while, so please, don't make this any harder than it has to be. We're not getting back together." I softened my tone in that last sentence, trying to make her see that this wasn't the way things were to work out but she threw back a fireball that I really did not expect.

"You know, Nick, I thought you'd see things more clearly after your little bit of fun last night. I thought you'd realise that I'm the one that's meant for you, but once again you're blind to the truth. That little bitch you dry humped on the dance floor last night was nothing more than a skanky Ravens End under the radar slut. You're blind to that, of course, because you're out to hurt the people that really love you." Her face was redder than a ripe tomato while it contorted into a spiteful grimace.

"Excuse me? How do you even *know* about last night? And for your information, little miss perfect, I did not 'dry hump' anyone. It's a little twisted that you spy on me and create your own little story about what happened. Real mature." I stood up, fuming. How could she spy on me like that?

"I didn't spy: I'm not twelve. Matty saw you down at Fivers and sent me a video. She was clearly scum Nick, what were you thinking? I guess I can forgive you though." She smiled, reaching out and making a grab for my hand.

"Sasha is not a slut and she's not scum. You know nothing about her and Matty had no right to film me. We are broken up and you need to deal with it Jenna. Please leave."

She sighed angrily, making her way to the door. "You'll soon realise how much you need me," she growled slightly through gritted teeth before leaving. I shook my head and pulled out my phone, messaging Sasha on complete impulse.

'Want to meet up?'

'That stressful, huh? Sure, where?'

'Outside Fivers? Half an hour?'

'Cool, I'll be there.' I smiled to myself, feeling relieved that she'd replied and not just deleted me thinking I'm some kind of creep.

I drove to Fivers, not really feeling the walk and sat on the wall in front of the venue to wait for Sasha.

She arrived around ten minutes later, an apologetic look on her face. "I'm so sorry," she said. "Kate, uh, my best friend, called me and wanted to chat. I didn't want to give her another reason to grill me so I couldn't tell her where I was going, which meant I had to have a valid excuse for getting off the phone." Her eyes darted about wildly, genuinely panicked about the fact she'd arrived so late.

"It's okay," I chuckled. "I haven't been here long. So, what did your friend want to chat about?" I asked, trying to start an easy conversation. This was the first time we'd ever spoken more than a few words to each other in person.

"Just about some guy she met somewhere or the other. Nothing new for Kate, to be fair or any of my other friends. Last night was a shock to them. I'm not usually so reckless. At least not when it comes to guys." She smiled, linking her arm casually with mine as we walked aimlessly towards the seafront.

"Well, I'm glad to know you're not a serial club kisser."

"Mm, speaking of serial club kissers, how comes you wanted to meet? What happened with your ex?"

"She insulted me, asked to get back together, insulted you and then told me I'd realise I need her." I laughed at the sheer stupidity of my situation.

"Ooh, what did she say about me?" she teased. "Seriously though, are you okay? I know how difficult break ups can get."

"Yeah, I'm good; I thought she was the sweetest, kindest girl I'd ever met, up until the past few weeks. It's been a shock, but I'm glad I've seen it sooner rather than later I guess. Meeting you yesterday just made me sure I'd never go back to her. It broke the chain, I guess."

"Well, I'm glad I could be of assistance." She smiled, unlinking arms to sit on a low wall overlooking the beach.

"So what's your story balamory?" I asked, joining her. The tide was in, so the water almost came up to where our feet dangled. It was nice. Calm.

"I've not had a boyfriend for over two years. The last one didn't exactly set a good example," she told me.

"What happened?"

"He ended up being a massive cheater and eventually a stalker. He's the reason we moved to Stepford; I mean Ravens End." She smiled a little at her own joke and I laughed. Not many girls could get away with finding themselves funny, but she managed to pull it off, her ocean blue eyes twinkling in the fading light.

"How have I never seen you before?" I asked.

"You weren't looking I guess, just like I wasn't looking for you. We've probably crossed paths a thousand times and not noticed because we weren't looking for anything. Fate has a funny way of keeping things from you until you're ready to accept them. I think they call it kismet," she said wisely.

"So you believe in fate then?" I asked.

"Yeah." A smile played at the edges of her lips. "I also believe in taking chances. Want to go for a swim?" she asked, looking around her before slipping her hoodie and jeans off to reveal a white cotton vest top and a pair of purple shorts. Before I could say anything, she was jumping from the wall into the water and screaming a laugh of delight as the water lapped at her skin. I pulled my t-shirt over my head and hesitated before removing my jeans. We'd be in so much trouble if anyone saw us right now, but then I realised that no one was actually around. I folded my clothes and put them on the wall next to Sasha's, taking a moment to prepare myself before I jumped into the icy ocean water. I immediately got a mouthful of salt water and felt all of my muscles stiffen in the sudden change of temperature. Once I'd recovered from the general shock, Sasha splashed me playfully and started to swim towards the metal railing of the engulfed steps that usually led to a glorious stretch of beach. She was fast. Her arms and legs worked furiously to propel her forward, but it didn't seem to faze her in the slightest. She wasn't even out of breath when I caught up with her.

"Where did you learn to swim like that?" I asked, astounded.

"I used to swim twice a week, sixty lengths without fail. Unless I was on the brink of death, in which case I would take a week off." She grinned. Something in her smile and the way she was made me crazy in the best way.

"You are one strange woman," I breathed, putting my hands on her hips under the water as I found my footing on the sand below us.

"What a lovely complement," she breathed back, only waiting a second before closing the distance between our frozen lips. In that second, my heart beat faster than it ever had. The adrenaline started to pump through my veins and I was completely lost in the moment. The kiss chafed a little, creating a heat between our lips that wasn't unpleasant, and grew more pleasant still when Sasha wrapped her legs around me. In the water, she weighed nothing but that of a feather, whereas the sparks that flew between us carried the weight of the world. I'd never felt such a strong connection with someone before. I'd known Sasha less than twenty-four hours and she was already opening my life up to amazing new possibilities and pushing the boundaries of everything I'd ever known to be right. This girl was magical.

# CHAPTER FOUR
*Sasha*

Nick was absolutely charming. He didn't freak at my sense of humour and instead of treating me like some discarded mistake, he actually seemed as if he wanted to know more about me. I know the facts; it's not like I'm stupid. I should be forgetting about last night at the club and moving on, but something about Nick had me itching to find out more. He seemed perfect and didn't hide the fact he'd just broken up with someone. I must sound crazy, right? Feeling such a connection with a stranger after a dance and a kiss in a darkened club? I know how it sounds and I know how it'll look if word gets out, but I can't help but sit here thinking about how perfect his lips felt on mine, and how time seemed to just stop while we had our moment. It was like I had spent my whole life just waiting for those deep brown eyes to come into my life. The very first second I locked eyes with him, everything just seemed to fall into place.

Kate knocked on my door bearing donuts and coffee, snapping me out of my reverie for the second time in twenty four hours. I loved her for bringing me treats, but I knew the hours that would follow would be a torturous string of questions and answers that would make me feel squeamish and too in-touch with my emotions. She didn't even wait for me to open the box of donuts before she started quizzing me. "Oh. My. God. You need to tell me everything!" she exclaimed, almost throwing her coffee everywhere as she gestured too vigorously with her hands. I sighed. There was no way to stop Kate when she wanted to know something. She'd hold you hostage or tie you to a chair with a swinging light bulb over your head if she thought it would get some info out of you.

"What do you want to know?" I asked, rolling my eyes and taking a seat at the breakfast bar.

"Who was he, what was he like, did he kiss well, have you stalked him yet, does he have a girlfriend? The list is endless!" she squealed, busying around me until she finally decided to sit down, her fidgety excitement diminishing a tad as she did so.

"His name is Nick. I've added him on Facebook and we talked a little but I haven't had a chance to stalk his profile properly yet. He has an ex but he says that kiss wasn't a rebound, and yes, he definitely kisses well." I smiled smugly at that last part, feeling more than cocky as I remembered how expertly his mouth explored mine. Kate gasped and almost immediately grabbed my phone.

"What are you doing?" I asked, my eyes bulging as a wave of panic rolled over my skin. Kate was the kind of person who would message Nick and accidentally sabotage the whole thing before it started.

“Well, we need to find out about him, so if you’re not going to rush to do that, I will.” She grinned.

“At least let’s do it on the computer. The screen is bigger and we won’t have to crowd around my poor, defenceless phone.” I grabbed a second donut as we headed upstairs, taking the first, refreshing sip of my coffee at the same time and enjoying the jolt. I shivered, feeling re-energized. Kate rolled onto my bed while I fired up my computer, holding my hand out behind me to get my phone back while I waited for it to load. I typed my password quickly and opened up Facebook.

Within a matter of minutes, Kate and I had assumed the stalking position and were routing through Nick’s photos, statuses and wall posts. After re-living the tale of the night before a few times, and a successful half an hour of stalking, we knew what Nick’s ex looked like. She was gorgeous in the traditional way. Blonde, skinny, green eyes, fashion sense of a rich girl Barbie doll and the smile of a millionaire. I couldn’t judge. I knew better than to judge a book by its cover by now. However, that didn't stop Kate from ripping into every fake designer t-shirt Nick’s poor ex happened to wear, and I’ll admit, I wasn’t non-judgey enough not to laugh. We also knew that Nick spent a lot of time with a dude called CJ who was your traditional hot-guy type. Kate spent far too long drooling at photos that featured him, and we found out that his sister was Cat Lacey, the most famous, beautiful up and coming supermodel of the past three years. Kate and I both sighed longingly at the thought of being a supermodel and got side-tracked while we discussed what we thought the model life might be like.

Eventually, there was nothing left of Nick's profile to stalk and I was at a complete loss of what to do. Kate was leaving and I suddenly found myself feeling my heart sink as if a dead weight had been dropped on it, so I did the only thing I could think of to pick myself up. I messaged Nick. He told me his ex had turned up at his house, so we didn't get to chat much, but just the fact that he'd replied to me while he was clearly busy made me feel all giddy and warm inside. It phased me a little that his ex was pestering him but we'd really only had a quick snog in a club, I didn't have any claim to him.

I skipped down the stairs to make myself another coffee. My parents had bought me a personal coffee maker for my birthday and, well, let's just say I put the thing to extremely good use. I danced a little on the spot as I put some milk in a saucepan to boil and added some cinnamon and cocoa powder to the mix, stirring it slowly with a whisk, until my mug had been filled by my coffee machine. I poured the cinnamon-chocolate milk into the coffee and added a little sugar to my weird little drink. I grabbed an old paperback from one of my many shelves on the hallway bookcase and sat at the island with it. The pages were seriously dog-eared, covered in coffee stains and inky scrawls in the margins. The scrawls were the reason no-one ever wanted to borrow books from our family. There were ideas, theories and guesses as to what would happen throughout the books. There were also reminders and doodles that always made me smile when I re-read them.

I was completely engrossed in the fictional world of my book when my phone chimed. It took a moment to shake myself of the last words I'd read before I could focus on the name that had appeared on the screen. It was Nick. I almost threw my phone across the room in excitement when I learned that he wanted to meet up, making squealing sounds as my mind reeled with possibilities. I finally calmed down enough to arrange when and where to meet, feeling the adrenaline start to pump through my veins. I ran upstairs and pulled on an oversized black hoodie and some holey skinny jeans over my vest top and shorts. I grabbed my trusty white converse and pulled them on clumsily, ignoring the frayed laces tangling up as I ran back down the stairs, tripping as I went, in too much of a hurry to be sensible. I took my keys from behind my favourite book on the book case and headed to the car. I was about to start the engine when Kate called. I cursed as I banged the steering wheel with my fist and answered the phone with what I hoped was a calm sounding voice. "What's up Kate?" I asked, ignoring the heavy thumping of my heart.

"Hey, I just wanted to tell you about this guy I just met. He's super hot and I thought you'd want to hear about him before I see where things go." She paused, leaving me enough time to tell her I was kind of busy, and then shrugged off my excuses. Ten minutes later, I was leaving way later than I had expected and every shred of excitement I had before had turned into bubbling anxiousness that was making me feel queasy.

I parked behind Fivers and ran back around to the front to meet Nick. I apologised for my tardiness and hoped he hadn't noticed the thin sheen of sweat that had glazed my face after running from the car park. After a walk and a little flirting, we ended up sitting on the long wall that stretched along the beach. A sudden impulse took over my mind and before I could really think things over, I was jumping into the water in only my vest and shorts.

The water pulled me under, and I felt electrified as the icy ripples consumed my body like jaws of blue liquid. The waves bit at my skin and in all honesty, I felt more alive than I had in a long time. Nick seemed to take forever to join me, as if he was wondering if he should just walk away before he got into something too daring. However, once he was actually in the water and the shock of the cold had died down, he seemed to relax, so I splashed him and swam off, racing my way towards to the metal railing of the would-be steps to the beach. Nick appeared soon after, sounding surprised at my swimming ability. I had swum to take my mind off of things for years, but I wouldn't put that information on him right now. I told him about my old swimming excursions. "You are one strange woman," he whispered throatily, resting his hands on my waist as he pulled me towards him. Every single thought in my head jumbled into one until I was too confused to do anything but thank him for the compliment and kiss him before my better judgement kicked in. I wrapped my legs around him in the water, and let him take me to a wonderful place that I was starting to think might be kissing heaven. I was starting to associate this feeling with Nick. We pressed ourselves together as if we were trying to mould ourselves into one person. I should have been shivering but being in his arms made me feel like I was on fire in the most excruciatingly emotional way. Eventually, the kiss ended and I sighed, putting my forehead to his and grinning with him as we both breathed heavily, water dripping from our hair and noses. I pulled away to look at him, caressing his face with one hand as the other held onto his shoulder. His eyes seemed to hold a thousand secrets that I couldn't wait to hear about. I wanted to know everything about him and I wanted him to know everything about me. Last night, in the club, I'd experienced true love at first sight and I felt as if I needed to pursue this strange turn of events and follow fate wherever it led me. I pecked Nick's lips lightly and started to untangle myself from him. "Do you want to come back to mine by any chance?" he asked. "Just to talk, I mean." He grinned sheepishly, looking down at the shimmering water.

"That sounds perfect," I laughed as I pushed off from the railing and swum back to the wall. Nick hoisted himself up and then reached down to help me up. We both pulled our clothes back on while we shivered, soaking them through with our wet skin as we walked hand in hand to the car park, meeting a dilemma when we realised we had both driven. I told Nick I'd follow him, getting into my car and turning the heat on full to warm myself up and dry off my clothes a little. It didn't work. I followed Nick to his flat, feeling butterflies, jitters and a heated wave of excitement rising through my body as we left our cars and headed up to his place.

Nick offered me a cup of coffee and I accepted far too slowly to be considered normal for me. He also offered me a change of clothes, which I tried to thank him for casually. Deep down I think my internal squeal was a little too obvious. He showed me to his bathroom, which had a very aqua theme to it and I removed my sodden clothes to swap them with his grey sweatshirt that was a little large, and a pair of cutely colourful boxers that fit me like shorts. He apologised for his lack of decent clothing when I emerged from the bathroom, but I told him it was fine, settling onto his worn leather sofa as if it were my own.

I felt so comfortable here. The books that littered every available surface ranged from classics to encyclopaedias to thrillers and his collection of DVDs was incredible. I was a little disappointed when I didn't see any music, but before I could comment on the lack of it, Nick seemed to notice his bad manners and told me to follow him if I wanted to see where he kept his music. He opened a door about half way down his hallway, right in between his kitchen and his bathroom. If it hadn't been for the wall to wall, floor to ceiling shelves that took up two entire walls and were filled with CDs, Vinyl and tapes, I probably would have been alarmed that he'd taken me to his bedroom. His taste was a little more than eclectic and I couldn't help but stare in awe of the sheer immensity of it. I flopped down onto his bed before I could even register what I'd done and began to search the shelves for CDs I owned or artists I knew of. I could yell snap for half of his collection but I knew that actually yelling 'snap' would make me look a little like a weirdo. "You are actually my hero right now," I admitted, seriously fascinated by his flexible taste.

"I'm no Enrique," he laughed, winking as he sat down beside me. "So, do you want to listen to something, I'll let you pick whatever you want," he grinned. I nodded and stood up to inspect the shelves. I was about to pick up a soundtrack when I noticed an entire shelf of mixes. I picked the first one, which dated back seven years, and thrust it at Nick. He groaned.

"Are you serious?" he asked, going a little red.

"Entirely." I smiled, watching him, fixated as he opened a cabinet opposite his bed to reveal a sound system that probably cost more than my car. It was only when he pressed play on the mix that I realised he had speakers mounted in all four corners of his room. I laid back on his bed, not caring how informal I was being and laughed when he turned off the main light to reveal glow in the dark stars on his ceiling. "Are you five?" I laughed, shaking my head when he nodded.

He laid down beside me and looked up at his little stars, whispering to me in the darkness. "When I first moved here, I was so relieved to be away from home but I suddenly felt really overwhelmed and alone. When I was young, I had glow in the dark stars and dinosaurs all over the ceiling in my bedroom. My dad had put them up when he and my mother first started fighting. He told me that if I felt scared, I could put my music on and look up at the stars and T-Rexs because as long as they still glowed, I'd be okay. I didn't sleep on my first night here because there were no stars, so I went out the next day and bought some. They've been here ever since." He looked at me out of the corner of his eye, gauging my reaction.

"Why did your parents fight?" I asked, determined not to let my face betray the sorrow I felt for him at that moment.

"Let's not ruin a good night," he whispered, turning onto his side to look into my eyes. "We'll save that for another time." He stroked my face softly before edging closer. He pressed his lips to mine softly and closed his eyes when I responded, needing this moment as much as he did. His hands lingered on my face as mine moved up and down his spine slowly, softly. We stayed like that for a while, not needing to make the moment anything more than what it was. Eventually, while the music floated softly through the air, and the stars on the ceiling glowed down, we fell asleep in each other's arms.

*

I woke up the next morning feeling warm and fuzzy. I was lying on top of sheets that were not my own, still in Nick's sweatshirt and colourful boxers, Although the smell of clean linen and forests after rain that I had come to associate with Nick in the past two days still lingered on his sheets, the man himself was nowhere to be seen. I wiped my eyes groggily and sat up, eventually swinging my legs over the side of the bed so that I could stand up and stretch. I walked down the hallway, following the delicious scent of sizzling bacon, and stopped when I found the source of deliciousness. Nick was standing by his kettle, fully dressed and waiting for it to boil, while two plates of bacon, eggs and toast sat on the counter beside him. "Oh, you're awake," he mumbled, sounding a little disappointed. "I was going to bring you breakfast," he pointed to the plates with a bright smile on his face that made my heart flip.

"I'm sorry I spoiled your surprise," I grinned back.

"It's okay," he laughed, bringing the food to his kitchen table. "I'm sure it'll taste just as bad at a table as it would in bed."

"I'm sure it's *delicious,*" I smiled, half hoping I was right, which I was. I moaned a little too enthusiastically at the high quality of his cooking and felt myself blush. "This is really tasty," I said around a mouthful of bacon as I pointed my fork towards him.

"I'm glad you like it," he laughed, setting down our coffee and digging in.

Once breakfast was over, Nick let me use a spare travel toothbrush and didn't bat an eyelid when I went to his bathroom to change and only gave him back his boxers. I made myself at home on his couch, sighing a little too audibly when he threw his arm casually around my shoulders and turned on the TV. We spent a lot of the day talking and chilling out. Everything just felt so comfortable and beautifully normal. We pecked at each other's lips occasionally and slipped into a deliciously romantic make out session at one point, but we didn't once discuss the fact that we'd only just met or the fact that we knew next to nothing about each other. I hadn't even asked him about his famous and absolutely gorgeous super model sister, but something in my gut told me that I'd have plenty of time to do that and to learn about him. Nothing about the way we'd met was normal, but that's what made it so special in my mind.

I left Nick's at about seven in the evening after a worried call from my mum and seven texts from Kate asking why I was suddenly MIA. When I got home, my mother hugged me tightly and asked where I had been. She didn't seem satisfied when I told her I was with a friend and started to quiz me about my 'new' boy-smelling sweatshirt. Eventually, I told her I'd met someone, but that only put more fear into her than she'd had when she thought I was missing. She asked me how long I'd known him and if he'd shown any tendencies towards stalking. I told her I wasn't going to make the same mistake twice and excused myself to take a shower and phone Kate. I was suddenly overwhelmed with tiredness, so I told Kate I'd talk to her tomorrow, and before I could even think of doing anything else, I was dreaming of unicorns and rainbows, or something equally girly and glittery.

# CHAPTER FIVE

*Nick*

Sasha and I didn't get a chance to see each other over the next few days. Life took a dramatic turn of events when my sister turned up at my front door with two black eyes and a cut the size of the Great Wall of China running into her hairline.

"What the hell happened?" I asked furiously. Let me tell you, seeing your little sister beat up and in joggers instead of her usual couture (or so I'm told) and face full of makeup is a big shock.

"Paulo was a fake, a fraud, a disaster and a terrible mistake," she cried; pushing past me dramatically and wheeling her pink suitcase into the living room.

"Yes, of course you can come in Cat! And I am just *great*, thanks so much for asking!" I rolled my eyes and slammed the front door before I followed her.

"Don't get sarky with me old man. I seriously need to crash here. I hate bodyguards and the only place Paulo won't find me before they find him is here. He doesn't know you exist, so, right now, my black eyes are off the map."

"Let's circle back to the black eyes and Paulo in just a sec. You didn't tell him you have a brother?"

"Well you don't tell people anything about the family; I figured you wouldn't want people knowing about you." She smiled and took her shoes off, leaving them by the armchair that she always occupied when she turned up.

"Okay, I'll give you that. So, Paulo?"

"He's not an actor. He's not anything and that doesn't even matter to me. I didn't know if he was an actor when I met him; I just *liked* him. He didn't have to lie. Not that it matters now because he turned out to be a stalker who doesn't like to be told he's a liar. The agency wanted to give me bodyguards. I told them I had a safe house to go to and gave them your mobile number, so I can go back when they find him. Everything I own is in the back of this safe car they gave me." She smiled sadly and turned the TV on, plopping down onto the sofa, clearly not interested in talking any more. I nodded, knowing better than to push her to talk.

"Fine, stay but don't tell our mother you're here."

"You know I won't. Where's Jen?" she asked. Crap. I guess news doesn't actually travel outside of Ravens End.

"We broke up," I told her. She didn't even look shocked when she gave me the generic, "I'm sorry, plenty of fish" speech. She did look shocked when I told her I thought I'd met someone else.

"This quickly?! This is *bound* to be good," she laughed. "Tell me."

I prepared myself to tell her all about Sasha. I sorted the words in my head and I was one hundred percent ready to explain everything when my phone sounded and I knew exactly who it was going to be. My mind melted, went cloudy and filled with all of the words that had passed between that beautiful girl and myself since we'd met and I couldn't quite remember what it was I had wanted to say. I figured it was best to just explain it like it is, instead of coming up with a huge speech, so I rambled. "I met her at Fivers about a week ago, maybe a little less. We just hit it off straight away and we *get* each other. She's fun, she's spontaneous, she makes the worst jokes and we've had a laugh so far. We haven't been on a proper date or anything yet and we barely know each other but she fills up my head and I don't have to think about what I'm saying when I'm with her. I can be myself, and she's just amazing, kind of crazy, and a little over the top, but she's just got this weird way about her that makes her irresistible." I sat down and let out a long breath. Cat smiled unexpectedly and clapped her hands together.

"Thank god you've found someone interesting for once! When do I get to meet her?" she asked. I suddenly felt on edge. Sasha and I hadn't even spent more than a couple of days together; did I really want to bombard her with the celebrity of my sister? I sighed. I knew she could handle it, and I didn't want her to think I didn't want her to meet my family or anything. Not that anyone should expect to meet someone's family after less than a week.

"I'll ask her now," I muttered, walking into the bedroom to give her a call, knowing I was destined to forever be under the command and spells of the women in my life.

She answered on the third ring."Are you expecting me to be nice to you, answering the phone all laughter and sunshine when you haven't replied to my text yet?" she joked. I could hear the smile in her voice and it made the corners of my mouth curve up involuntarily. It made me feel warm.

"Actually, I have a really weird request." I held my breath, waiting to see if she'd say anything before I carried on.

"I'm nodding, but you can't see me, so uh, go ahead."

"Okay, my sister is in town," I heard a sharp intake of breath on Sasha's end of the phone and carried on. "She, uh, wants to meet you, I think, and she said soon, and your message asked if I wanted to meet up tonight, so I was wondering if you wanted to come over and meet my sister?" I asked.

Sasha squealed uncharacteristically and then suddenly caught herself with a cough. "Yeah, I'll come over, give me half hour?" she said, clearing her throat as if trying to act cool. I laughed and told her I'd see her then. I suddenly felt self-conscious. My sister wasn't exactly your regular human being and, well, she has no boundaries either. My palms started to sweat and I couldn't think straight. Had I just made the biggest mistake? Sasha and I hadn't had a chance to get to know each other yet, and now she was about to meet my sister. I'm pretty sure I'm crazy. I tried to tell Cat to keep it toned down. I asked her to try not to be so, well, 'famous' but she waved me off and when the doorbell finally rang, she rushed to the door before I even had a chance to stand up. I could hear Cat greeting Sasha from the living room and realised this was all too late to fix and so I might as well enjoy watching my own little world burn to the ground.

*

Maybe I over-reacted a little. Sasha and Cat actually seemed to get on really, really well. I wasn't sure if I should be pleased about it or not, considering I barely got a word in edgeways. Cat and Sasha got wrapped up talking about makeup, moisturisers, eyeliners and random designers with names I'm pretty sure are made up. I just sat there, admiring the mystery girl that hadn't even been in my life for a week, talking to my sister like she'd known her for years and looking completely in place in my life. I watched her little movements and learned her tells.

I watched her hand brush her hair back behind her ears as she listened intently, I watched her fingers clench at her knees when something made her uncomfortable and I watched her eyes widen and light up when something she was thinking of made her happy. Was it completely crazy to believe this could actually work? My head told me it was, that you couldn't possibly fall in love with a stranger, but when Sasha turned her head and smiled shyly at me, only holding my eyes for a second or two, my head didn't matter, because the thumping in my heart was the only thing I could think about. Why shouldn't I pursue something I feel so strongly about? My head once again stepped in and told me a thousand different reasons but I ignored them, for now anyway.

"So, what are you doing with your life Sasha?" Cat asked. "Where do you want to be in ten years?" I frowned at my sister, but she ignored me, as per usual.

"Well, I'm in college right now. I've got two months left. Most of my friends have left already but because I started late, when I moved here, I mean. I have to finish the time I missed in the beginning, so I'm just hanging around there until I've finished up. I'm lucky enough that my best friend switched courses around the same time that I joined, so I'm not the only one finishing at an awkward time. I work in the Waterstones in town, and I'd really like to be a writer." Sasha blushed and I felt chills go up my spine. This girl is perfect.

"Oh, Nick is a lecturer at East College! This is so cute! What are your subjects?" Cat asked her. It suddenly sunk in that I didn't know what college Sasha went to. I panicked, feeling the nerves and anxiety rise and bubble under my skin because I didn't know if we were even allowed to be seeing each other. Sure, she's eighteen, but it's got to be frowned upon to be dating a student, even if they don't take your subject.

I found myself asking, "What college do you go to?" I couldn't even disguise the worry in my voice.

"I take English Language, English Literature and Art, and uh, South, why?" It seemed to dawn on her just after she asked why and her bright eyes widened then her fingers gripped at her knees as if they were the edge of a cliff.

"They're really cool subjects. You're good at art? How are you with makeup?" Cat asked, pausing when she saw that Sasha and I were looking at each other with slightly relieved expressions. "Have I missed something here?"

"Nick didn't know I was at college, I didn't know Nick was a lecturer. We could've been breaking some rules I suppose, but we're not even in the same college district so I guess that was just a close call. And yeah I'm pretty good with makeup, why?" Sasha fidgeted in her seat a little and I finally did what I'd wanted to do all night. I sat by her side and took her hand. Maybe she'd stop fidgeting so much. She smiled gratefully at me and Cat 'Aww'd' us patronisingly.

"You guys are too cute. Basically, once my face has healed, I was thinking of getting a few new head shots for my portfolio. If you're good with makeup and you're interested, you could totally make my face look fancy." I smiled. Cat had always been a kind soul at heart, and I was glad she was warming up to Sasha so thoroughly. She'd never have asked Jenna to do her makeup. Jenna and Cat had battled through a strained relationship. Cat thought Jenna was controlling but tolerated her and Jenna thought Cat was too free spirited, which really attested to Jenna's small mindedness now I think back on it.

"I could have a go now if you want, we could see if we can cover those bruises, do a few test designs, see if you like them before you actually hire me. I wouldn't want you to hate me for messing up your face."

"Yeah, that sounds great! I'll get my makeup!" Cat squealed, running out of the front door to what was the agency's idea of a safe car. It wasn't exactly inconspicuous, so I wondered if the agency had actually used their brains while choosing it.

“I’m sorry about her,” I said, shaking my head.

Sasha giggled melodically and kissed me softly. “I’ve wanted to do that all night,” she whispered huskily against my lips, closing her eyes and kissing me again. She tasted of strawberries and the blackcurrant chewing gum that she always chewed. I felt like I could never get enough of that taste until my sister coughed awkwardly as she re-entered the room laden with cases and bags. Our moment of bliss was cut off. Sasha blushed and asked where was best to set up. I told her that the kitchen would be fine and she followed Cat out there with me trailing behind. Sasha gasped at the sheer amount of makeup that Cat carried with her on a daily basis, and practically fainted when she said she’d be right back with the rest. Sash opened the many boxes and examined the many, many strange looking pots and brushes.

“I’m so out of my league with this,” I groaned, throwing my hands up in defeat. Sasha laughed as she squirted some nude coloured liquid onto the back of her hand.

“You could grab a beer and watch TV, you know, do manly things with your time or whatever,” she teased, winking at me. All I wanted to do at that moment was show her exactly how manly I could be, but right now, we’d have to settle for stolen kisses and short-lived glances, because there was only room for one big story in my flat at a time, and right now, that story was Cat.

Eventually, Cat and Sasha had settled on several facial designs that apparently worked beautifully with Cat's complexion and facial structure. I thought Sasha's art work was beautiful but I didn't understand how it would benefit anyone whilst it was on Cat's face. They took several photos so that they could remember the designs at a later date and then started to pack everything away. "I'm going to take a shower and get all this makeup off." Cat smiled, heading to the bathroom and finally giving us some privacy.

"So, that was the weirdest few hours of my life," I muttered, clearing away some glasses that I'd left on the draining board.

"Your sister is nice. She's way more down to earth than I'd expected. She is a super model after-all." She wrapped her arms around my waist and rested her cheek on my back as I reached up to put the glasses in the cupboard. I turned to hug her back properly and we just stayed there for a while, taking in whatever it was that was going on between us. I never wanted to let her go and the thought of her running off with another guy was suddenly the most infuriating idea on the planet.

"I've got work tomorrow, but do you want to meet up for lunch?" I asked.

Sasha pulled away and smiled at me mischievously.

"You mean like a date?"

"I guess." I smiled.

"Hmm, well, I suppose I could check my schedule." She looked up through thick lashes and dropped her gaze again as she pulled out her phone. "I could fit you in at around one-ish, if you're around then," she said in what sounded like a painfully accurate Ravens End accent.

"That's perfect. I'll meet you outside the East College at one then." She grinned at me for a moment and sighed, hugging herself closer to me again. She told me she had to get going and gave me the most bittersweet kiss before she turned to leave. This girl was going to be the absolute death of me.

Cat rambled on about how great Sasha was for the rest of the night before it was finally time for me to get some sleep. I was thankful for the silence when I laid on top of my covers, under those plastic stars and fell asleep wondering what tomorrow would bring and if it would be a make or a break in the weirdness that was my new love life.

In the morning, Cat was already settled in front of my TV with a coffee and a bowl of cornflakes. "Make yourself at home," I muttered. She flipped me off and went back to her early morning episode of beauty and the geek. I sighed and left for work. I picked CJ up on the way and I was dreading how he'd react when I told him Cat was currently sitting in my living room, so I decided to just rip the plaster off and do it straight away. At first, his face was blank and unreadable, and then out of nowhere, he was asking questions upon questions about what had happened to her. After I explained the very little of what I did know, CJ asked me to turn the car around. I regretfully declined. "We have to get to work CJ, besides, what do you think will happen? It's not like you haven't tried to get her to like you before and it didn't go so well the last time." I shook my head, smiling at the memory of CJ in suits and ties, bearing gifts of chocolate, flowers and makeup in the wrong shades.

"Just because I got it wrong last time, doesn't mean I'll get it wrong this time, okay?" he huffed childishly, folding his arms over his chest petulantly. I told him I'd seen better men try and he punched me hard in the arm, which I'll admit I did deserve. We pulled into the college car park and forgot all about our conversation when we saw Jenna's pink KA parked in my space. She really wasn't going to give up.

"Great," I muttered. We found another space and headed into the building, telling a few students to find their passes before the barrier attendant caught them and gave them a hard time. We remembered how irritating the attendant's lectures on passes had been when we'd been students. They weren't pretty. "Why the hell is Jenna here?" I whispered to myself, puzzled.

"God knows mate, isn't she supposed to be teaching at South?" CJ replied.

"Wait, she's been teaching at South the whole time Sasha has been there? You don't think they know each other do you?"

"God, I hope not, that would be really bad luck for you man. Speaking of, how are things going with your little hottie?" CJ grinned slyly and slapped my back. I sighed, telling him all about the night we went swimming, to the interrogation from Cat to our lunch date. CJ nodded along and made sleazy comments that I tried my best to ignore right up until we got to my classroom. I smiled at the familiar room. The rotating board that alternated between black and white, with the pens, chalks and erasers in pots that were screwed to the frame on either side. The smart board that sat mounted on the wall beside it that I mainly used to show films of the books my students were supposed to be reading at home. The heavy, mahogany desk with the seven hundred year old computer that frustrated me to no end, and the bookcase that held all of my favourite classics and several other good reads that I'd lend to students occasionally if they were showing outstanding merit. It all felt like a home away from home. I locked the door behind me as CJ turned to enter his own classroom, which sat beside mine with only a thick glass wall in between, and started to rifle through the papers in my desk draws to find the emergency lesson plans I'd written before the summer. I thanked my past self for knowing I'd end up not writing them over the holidays. I smiled to myself. I will be teaching Romeo and Juliet for the first month of the term. My favourite.

My first class of the day was absolutely brilliant. The students were engaged and interested, taking in my words as if they were the secrets of the world and involving themselves in debates about the underlying meaning in the words of William Shakespeare. The lecture left me feeling like I'd done something great and reminded me why I'd wanted to teach in the first place. The lesson lead right up until lunch time and I'd been so wrapped up in it that I went over my time, causing reception to send Sasha up to my classroom with a visitor's pass. I grinned at her and let my poor captives go, telling them that they'd have no homework until their next lesson, and hoping that they wouldn't think anything of the beautiful girl standing at my door.

After my last student had left, Sasha stepped into the room and beamed at me. "This classroom is amazing," she whispered, ignoring my open arms to study the book shelves behind me.

"More amazing than me?" I joked, grinning easily at her. She tried to hide her smile but failed, walking slowly back around the desk with a bright spark in her eyes to step into my arms. I leaned forward and pressed my lips lightly to hers.

"Hi," I said softly. I didn't know I'd regret it later.

# CHAPTER SIX

*Sasha*

Nick's lips tasted like sweetness and coffee. He made me sigh like a sappy girly girl and I hated that fact, almost as much as I loved it. "Sorry, my lesson over ran," he mumbled against my lips. I let him lure me into a deeply passionate kiss that would have had even the sluttiest girls gasp. When we broke away, Nick kept his eyes closed like a dork and whispered, "Woah." I just laughed and waved him off, taking his hand as we walked out of the classroom.

We ended up hiding out on the top floor of a dingy KFC. It wasn't the most romantic date but it suited our already dysfunctional relationship. Nick kept seeing his students as we walked down the high street, so he lead us down a few side roads until we hit some lecturer-friendly back streets. "I know walking into students is inevitable but the questions that get asked once they see you are relentless and it gets annoying. It's like they see you on the street and suddenly realise you have a life outside of that tiny little classroom." He sighed, causing me to giggle. I was actually kind of enjoying how low-key and normal this date was. Nick smiled at me from across the table and I couldn't help but blush. This was the first time I'd been able to look at him properly, without distractions, and see him for who he was. I really liked what I saw. He was kind, intelligent, absolutely hilarious, definitely not afraid of what other people thought of him, and incredibly beautiful, inside and out. Every accidental touch, every smile, and every glance made me feel as if I was on fire. I'd never felt this way before and I wasn't really sure how to take it. "How's Cat?" I asked, conversationally, trying to keep my cool.

"She's great actually. Couldn't stop going on about how you're an incredible makeup artist. She asked me if I'd mind if she hired you as her personal stylist," he laughed, popping a chip into his mouth.

"What did you tell her?"

"Well, I said I couldn't possibly relinquish such a beautiful girl, and she'd just have to find another amazing person to be her personal beauty slave."

"Ah man, I could've done with the escape. You see there's this guy that kissed me in this club, and he just seems to keep appearing," I joked, making Nick snort a little.

"Ah, that sounds like the situation I have with this stalker girl. She's a little crazy and made me jump into the ocean the second time I met her."

"She sounds like an absolute psycho; maybe you shouldn't get yourself involved with her."

"I think it's too late; she's got me acting crazy to be honest," he admitted. I grinned in response, feeling my cheeks redden as Nick leaned forward. He pressed his lips to mine softly, causing my eyes to flutter closed before he deepened the kiss. His lips became more domineering as he pulled me onto his lap. My head felt fuzzy and light, taking in every second of this moment. The taste of his lips, the heat of his breath, and the graze of his teeth as they nibbled on my bottom lip occasionally had me wishing we weren't in a public place. We eventually pulled away from each other, letting our eyes meet, and our sheepish grins turn into quiet laughter.

"I really could get used to this," I warned, running my fingers through his short, wavy hair briefly.

"Me too."

I walked with Nick back to his campus and followed him up to his classroom. When we got there, he went to sit in his fancy leather chair and I hoisted myself up onto his desk in front of him. He pulled himself forward, resting his arms either side of me as we talked. Things with Nick felt so comfortable and real, not like those daydreams where you wished this stuff would happen, but the real thing; flesh and blood, right in front of my eyes. It made me feel fluttery and jittery and good.

Nick's first student arrived early and I could see he felt uneasy about whatever gossip the crazy girl sitting on his desk would bring, so I told him I was late to meet Kate and made a quick exit. Once I was out of the building, I felt strangely unfulfilled. We hadn't really gotten to say goodbye, no kiss, no hug, no plans for next time. I huffed, making my way to my car.

I'd put myself in a bad mood by the time I'd gotten home. I'd been so worried about making sure Nick was happy that I'd not thought about goodbyes and plans; I cursed myself for being stupid and stalked moodily up to my room to inbox Kate.

'Kate, Nick makes me floopy,' I typed.

'Why, what did he do?!'

'He didn't do anything, I'm just all messed up over him. This makes me feel girly and stupid and blah.'

'Want me to come over? We can chat. Besides, I need to see a girly Sasha.'

'Yes, bring me some salted popcorn? I'll give you the money when you get here?'

'Sure thing, see you soon :)'

I pulled my knees up to my chest and pulled up my unfinished Jane Eyre Essay. I only had a few more paragraphs left to write and I knew I'd be done by the time Kate arrived. My new found appreciation for the weirdness of life really helped me wrap up the essay and form a strong conclusion. I felt as if I'd gotten my writing mojo back, and even though I was still in a mood with myself, I was glad. I didn't even know if this essay would need to be handed in anymore, considering we were getting a new lecturer, but I wanted to finish it anyway.

Kate arrived with my popcorn and we headed straight up to my room to discuss my new found and extremely irritating girliness. "First of all Sash, how the hell could you forget to tell me that you did *Cat Lacey's* makeup?! That must have been *amazing*. We are definitely circling back to that. I want her to be my best friend. So tell me, young padewan, what are you feeling?" Kate joked. I rolled my eyes and started to tell her, just letting the words flow as they popped into my brain.

"I don't even know. He makes me feel light headed and amazing like anything is possible and as if I'm the only girl on this god-damn planet. He makes me laugh so much I swear I could spray water out of my nose, and he makes me nervous, so, so nervous and dorky. My palms sweat, my legs feel like jelly, but as soon as I'm in his arms, I'm okay again, like I didn't know there was a piece of me missing until I met him. He fills a void I didn't know existed and ugh, I just don't know." I put my head in my hands and rubbed my face in frustration.

Kate smiled sympathetically at me and laughed. "Sash babes, it sounds like you're a little bit in love."

"Don't be silly. I can't possibly be in love; I only just met the guy," I sighed, thinking over everything that had happened so far, everything I'd felt in this short amount of time and how not saying goodbye had affected my mood so drastically. "Oh god, I'm in love," I admitted, flopping onto my bed and groaning into a pillow. I flipped over and faced the ceiling. "Love sucks, Kate. You're better off carrying on with your multiple suitors." Kate laughed and checked her phone.

"Do you want to know why I keep jumping from guy to guy?"

"Go on," I prompted, not quite sure where this was leading.

"I fell in love with a guy and he ended things with me about a week before you came to town, actually. The only reason I haven't settled down is that I've been trying to find the feeling again and I just can't. I know you opted to stay celibate until you found your Prince Eric, but I couldn't do that. If I did that, I'd just dwell on it all so much that I'd never do anything again," she sighed, texting someone.

Kate has always been honest, but I'd never imagined that the reason she wanted to sleep with every guy she met was that she was trying to fall in love. We talked a lot about Mr. Right and how we didn't know how on earth you were supposed to know who he was. We had college the next day so we turned in early. I don't think either of us actually got any sleep though. Kate tossed and turned on the trundle bed and I laid on my back, staring at my ceiling with no glowing stars to comfort me like the ones at Nick's. There was just the nagging memories of tonight's conversation about being in love and all kinds of other things playing on my mind. I didn't know if I was ready for love so soon.

I was far too tired by the time we got to campus that I wandered past the small Starbucks that stood on the corner of the main college building and it took a full five minutes for me to realise. I told Kate I had to go back for a coffee and she asked me to get her a frappe. I exchanged polite conversation with Dom, the well trained Barista that had been serving me since I'd arrived here and took the drinks over to the sugar station where I added a mound of sugar, some cinnamon, vanilla, nutmeg and chocolate to my latte. Today would be fuelled by coffee and sugar; there was no way around it.

My first lesson was long. It dragged on for what felt like hours and my lecturer seemed to be picking on me a hell of a lot. I knew exactly why. This new woman that had been sent in to take over our morning Lit classes was the same blonde that had been in almost all of Nick's Facebook photos. I felt queasy at the thought and by the end of the lecture, I had the most ridiculous headache and a strong urge to just go home to sleep. As I was getting up to leave, my lecturer called my name. "Miss Santiago, I'd like to have a word," she said sternly. I felt that awful sick feeling you get when you feel like you're going to be in trouble, even though you *know* you've done nothing wrong. I sat on the edge of my desk and waited for her to yell at me for whatever she'd decided I'd done. "I want to warn you, Sasha, that getting involved with a lecturer is a very, very bad idea," she growled.

"Excuse me?" I asked, feeling my palms sweat nervously.

"Don't play dumb. You're a very smart girl and you know it. I saw you and Nick Lacey getting cosy at the other college as if you have nothing to hide." She sounded so bitter and I wondered why. I probably shouldn't have asked; I should have engaged my brain before I started getting defensive.

"What's it to you, Miss Green? I'm an adult. I'm finished here in two months, and the colleges aren't even connected. There's nothing stopping us, so *why* is it such a problem for you?" I felt the corners of my mouth turn up into a smug smile and I kicked myself mentally. I may not have been in trouble before, but I certainly would be now. I shouldn't have antagonised her. I knew better.

"Not that it's any of your business, but up until recently, I was Nick's girlfriend. I know him better than he knows himself, so I know that his involvement with you is just a game to keep him occupied until something better comes along. You may not be doing anything wrong *technically*, but I'm sure the residents of Ravens End would be interested to know that a student and a lecturer are spending a hell of a lot of time together. They never need to know that you're not at the same colleges. Once the rumour is planted in their minds, they're bound to talk. Once they start an investigation into the mystery, you'd be surprised at how easy it'll be to make Nick Lacey look suspicious, and how would your parents feel about this little situation?" She smiled creepily, reminding me of a more twisted version of the Cheshire cat.

"My parents want me to be happy, they trust me, they don't care about gossip and scandals. As for the other threats, you sound like you still care about Nick; why else would you be threatening me? You wouldn't hurt him." I grimaced, feeling sick and clammy as I got up to leave. I swung my bag over my shoulder and rushed out of the building as quickly as I could.

Kate was waiting outside with a cinnamon latte and a frappe. "You don't look so good, and I'm sure I recognise that woman," she said in a high voice as she handed me my drink. "Do you want me to drive you home?" I nodded and handed her my keys, trying to breathe properly as we made our way to my car. "What did Green want?" she asked as she threw her bag onto the back seat of the car and stuck the key into the ignition.

"She's Nick's ex." I watched Kate's eyes widen and eyebrows go up as she realised exactly where she'd recognised her from. She asked me if I was okay, and when I explained what had happened, she told me I needed to phone Nick. I did, right there and then, and he told me to stop by his place. He didn't even mind that Kate was with me and that was why I liked him so much, he was so accommodating, so chilled. It made me wonder how he'd ever been in a relationship with someone as overbearing as Miss Green.

Kate tried not to fangirl over Cat, but she was soon interviewing her and god knows what else in the living room, so Nick and I went to the kitchen to talk. I told him what Jenna had said and tried my best to keep calm and not panic while he sat silently in front of me. I paced, he paced, and eventually, we both stopped. "This isn't good," he stated. I was hoping he'd have thought of some kind of solution after the pacing, but then I realised that I hadn't exactly been wracking my brains either.

"I don't know what to do. Maybe we should call it quits." I hugged myself, regretting what I'd said instantly, but knowing it was our only solid option for the moment. I was just kidding myself; I didn't want to call it quits at all.

"There's another way Sasha, there's got to be, we just have to find it. I'm not giving up on us when this is the *only* thing that has felt right in a long time," he huffed, switching on the kettle and pulling two mugs from a cupboard. "Coffee?" I nodded, taking the spoon from him and adding the right amounts of coffee and sugar to one of the mugs.

"I don't want to give up either, but she seemed so serious. I swear her eyes glowed red at one point." I smiled a little and Nick laughed.

"Are you one of those people who makes jokes in a crisis?" he asked. I nodded and he laughed again, reaching out to me and pulling me close. I breathed in his clean linen and rainy forest scent. I felt so safe, I felt at home, and I didn't want to have to let this go. Ever.

"What do we do?" I asked with more conviction than I had expected, leaning into his chest.

He stroked my hair comfortingly and whispered, "I'm not sure, but we'll figure it out." I squeezed him a little tighter, never wanting to let go, and felt grateful for Kate and Cat when they wandered into the kitchen, asking if Kate and I could stay for dinner and some movies.

We ordered Chinese food and Nick and I snuggled on the sofa while Kate and Cat sprawled out on the floor with blankets and pillows from Nick's boiler cupboard. I tried not to worry about the incident with Miss Green, but I could feel Nick's arms tense around me every time someone got a text or a message. He was just as worried about what she would do as I was and the difference was; he knew what she was capable of. Eventually, Cat told us we were fidgety and disturbing the film and suggested we get some rest while she and Kate stayed in their slumber party positions. The popcorn in a massive blue bowl between them was slowly emptying. Nick and I headed to his room. He gave me another sweatshirt and the boxers that he'd lent me before, telling me he'd set them aside with a shy grin on his face, and asked me if I wanted to choose a CD. I chose something that consisted of mainly slow, beautiful songs that would help us sleep easier and got into bed beside him.
"I don't want to lose you," I whispered into the darkness. Nick's arms encircled me and held me tight.

"You won't," he promised, kissing my forehead and closing his eyes.

My dreams were abstract but strangely terrifying. I didn't know what they were about, but I knew that I was scared of them. I woke up in the middle of the night feeling green. I headed to the bathroom and splashed water over my face. I felt so blurry and sick. Everything about this situation with Miss Green was making me so nervous and on edge. I doubted myself, I even doubted Nick, and I couldn't see a way out. I went back to bed and tried to be as quiet as possible as my breathing quickened and my head began to spin. Now wasn't a time for a panic attack. Nick opened one eye lazily. "Stop fretting, we'll figure this out Sash." I nodded as a tear ran down my cheek, causing Nick to sit up and run his fingers through his hair. "Hey, what's up?" he asked softly, stroking my back gently with his fingertips.

"I just don't know what to do," I sniffed, my voice cracking under the weight of the situation.

"We can't do anything tonight Sasha, but I'm going to sort this okay? For you, and for us, I'm going to figure this out."

"Okay," I whispered, turning to bury my face in his chest, needing to feel close to him and needing him to hold me. We stayed like that for a long time, him being strong, and me letting my guard down for once. Eventually, we lay back down and cuddled close, letting the night and the stress seduce us into deep, dreamless slumbers. The last thing I remember was Nick whispering, "We'll get through this." Then the world was finally silent.

# CHAPTER SEVEN

*Nick*

Sasha wasn't acting like herself over the next couple of days. Even Cat commented on it. She was still fun and she was still bubbly, but there was just something missing and none of us could put our finger on it. All I wanted to do was make her feel better. I knew she was anxious and I couldn't do anything to help her.

We were lying on the sofa, Sasha asleep and me reading, when it hit me. I knew exactly what I could do to help. I tried to sit up without waking her but she'd been sleeping lightly since the run in with Jenna. She yawned, rubbed her eyes and sat up. "What's up?" she asked groggily, curling her knees up to her chest.

"I'm going to sort this shit with Jenna out once and for all," I spat, letting the fiery anger I felt at Jenna fuel me.

"You've got an idea?" she asked, her voice less croaky now.

"Yes, and I'm hoping it will work. I hate seeing you so freaked out Sash," I admitted. She smiled sleepily, running her hand up my chest before kissing me softly.

"I like you a lot," she whispered, running her fingers through my hair and scratching softly at the side, like she knew I loved, before letting me go. I watched her change the channel and curl back up watching, "Down to you." Her obsession with Freddie Prinze Jr. was actually quite worrying.

I jumped in my car and drove to the South College. When I got there, they didn't even ask for my name at reception, they just sent me straight up to Jenna's classroom. I didn't bother knocking when I saw she was in the room alone. I just barged in and slammed the glass door behind me, making it rattle with the force. Jenna jumped but then smiled wickedly when she saw me. "I knew it wouldn't be long until *you* turned up, Mr. Romantic. To defend your lady's honour, I presume?" She lifted a stack of text books from her desk and carried them to a cupboard that joined the back of her room to the next one.

"I'm not here to defend anyone's honour. I'm here to ask you why the hell you're threatening Sasha," I breathed out, pinching the bridge of my nose to dispel the red spots of anger that were slowly appearing in my eyes.

"I didn't threaten her; I was offering friendly advice. We all know how unforgiving this town can be." She looked up at me, smiling as if nothing had happened.

"Only if someone makes a big deal out of it Jen. You know no one would have ground to stand on unless someone made up a few lies. It sounds like a threat to me and I don't think you should be threatening students."

"Oh Nick, so naïve. You don't get your way if you don't break a few rules, I thought you realised that?"

"You know I'm not breaking any rules. What the hell happened to you Jenna?"

" *You* happened to me. You ruined my life and now I'm going to ruin yours. We could've been happy, we could've moved in with each other, gotten married, had kids and everything would've been plain sailing, but instead, you wasted my time. Now I'm on the shelf, my parents are disappointed in me and even my sister has a better life. If you hadn't ended things, none of this would've happened. This is your own fault." She slammed her fist down on her desk, and the vein in her forehead started to bulge. She kind of looked like the hulk.

"We weren't working, we both knew it but you pushed too hard. Our relationship was on the rocks months before you told me you were moving into *my* flat without me even asking you to." I sighed, rubbing my temples. "How are you still on this? Why can't you see how toxic things got?"

"Oh, you are still hooked on that line? Why can't you admit that you got scared? I know you still love me. This thing you've got going with Santiago is just a cry for help. You need me. I know you do." She grinned manically, stepping forward and pressing her lips to mine. It felt so wrong and out of place. I pushed her away without a second thought and stepped back so that she couldn't do it again.

"I don't love you Jenna. I don't and I'm sorry but that's the way it is. I did once and it was great, but you have to let this go," I pleaded. This was not going well. Sasha needed this to go well. I cursed myself internally for thinking this could ever be a good idea. I should know better than anyone that there's no reasoning with Jenna when something's on her mind. I just wish she wasn't being so venomous. This wasn't the Jenna I'd known for years. Not at all.

"Nick, if you want this to go away, you know what you have to do. If you don't, well, there's the door," she sighed, almost as if she regretted what she was doing, but then again, if she did, she'd stop the madness.

"I can't tell you how disappointed I am. This is just more proof that you're not who you used to be. Have a nice life Jenna." I turned and walked away. We'd have to come up with another plan. I was dreading telling Sasha this was a bust.

When I got to my car, I slammed the door and drove straight to CJ's. Sash would be fine with her Freddie Prinze Jr films, and Cat would be home soon. I needed to brainstorm with my best mate.

When I got to CJ's, he was slumped at his desk with a stack of essays beside him. "Did these kids even realise they were taking Lit?" he asked, disbelief in his tone.

"Bad class?"

"First years," he sighed. "What's up? You look all frustrated. Beer?"

"Yeah please mate, I'm driving though so just the one. I have an issue."

"Go on," he prompted as he went to grab the beers.

"Jenna threatened Sasha, I tried to fix it and I think I might have made it worse."

"Jenna threatened Sasha? Christ, what a bitch," he muttered, handing me an essay and a red pen to mark it with. The least I could do was help him so I dragged one of his armchairs up to the opposite side of his desk and began to mark.

"Tell me about it. She's saying she'll start rumours, jeopardise my job and make us Ravens End lepers. I don't know what to do. Sasha's blaming herself, she's anxious and wound up, worrying about it all the time. I can't believe Jenna would do this to us. Sasha's her student for Pete's sake!" I finally burst. The pent up anger towards the whole situation had been boiling under the surface for days. I circled a spelling error and wrote the correct version of the word in the margin.

"Maybe I can talk to her?" CJ asked, laughing at a typing error on the essay he was grading.

"You could try but I don't know if it will help. I've only made it worse by trying to reason with her. She kissed me."

"She what?! How does Sasha feel about that?"

"I haven't spoken to her since I left the college; I'm telling her when I get home."

"She's practically living with you right now."

"I've got Sash, Cat and Kate all crashing at mine right now. I'd never admit it to them, but it's actually nice having the place full of people. I know me and Jenna broke up over her inviting herself to live with me, but I guess that just proves that it was the relationship that was the problem rather than the actual situation. I don't know. I feel like an awful person, but when it's right, it's right, you know?" I sighed, swigging my beer and grabbing another paper from his pile after giving one of his students a C.

"How about I come over tonight? A house full of chicks can't make you feel manly. We can have a guy's night and they can bugger off doing some girly shit. It'll give us time to brainstorm this situation with that woman as well," he grinned, handing me the paper he was grading that had actually gone so entirely off the subject that it was talking about another book.

"Nice one," I muttered. "Yeah, come over at around 6, the girls are probably sick of films by now anyway. Sasha and Kate are going to their respective homes tomorrow so they'll probably enjoy something a little different."

"I love how you've just invited Sasha's best friend into your life like it's no big; she could be an axe murderer."

"Her and Cat have taken a shine to each other and if Kate could be an axe murderer, so could Sash." I laughed as I headed towards the door.

"Good point. Well, I'll see you later man." He shut the door behind me and I drove straight home.

Sasha, Kate and Cat were all sporting gloopy, green face masks when I got home. They'd prepared an actual meal between them that actually smelled delicious and they'd also pooled their resources and done my food shopping for the week. "We felt bad for eating all your food," Sasha said smiling, patting my leg briefly from her cross legged position on the floor.

"CJ is coming over tonight, we haven't spent a lot of time together since we went back to work, so we're going to chill, and you guys seem set with what you're doing, so we'll keep out of your way," I announced before asking Sasha if I could have a word. She was wearing black pyjama shorts with little frogs all over them and an orange vest top. Even with green goo on her face, she looked irresistible.

"I think I made things with Jenna worse. I'm so, so sorry, but I really thought I was going to help. I thought she'd see reason," I sighed. Sasha rubbed my arms and told me it was okay, she hadn't expected it to go away overnight. "There's something else," I added, ignoring the alarmed look in her eyes. "Jenna kissed me. It was repulsive but she did it nonetheless." I watched several emotions play over her face in a matter of seconds. Hurt, confusion, denial, betrayal, and finally, anger.

"That bitch," she hissed. "That woman is going to have the worst karma when it comes around."

"You're not mad at me?" I asked, feeling slightly relieved.

"I saw first-hand how much she wanted us to break up Nick. I'm not stupid, and she thought it'd make me want you less. The fact you even told me proves you're so much better than her, and well, it kind of makes you irresistible," she grinned, reaching up to scratch the side of my head softly and kissing me on the cheek, her face got serious again then. "I am angry though; at her. She's vile Nick, I'm sorry but she is." I didn't disagree.

"I'm glad I met you," I stated, matter-of-factly.

"Me too," she smiled and wandered back to the living room. I heard Cat and Kate ask her what I'd said in hushed voices, and tried to not laugh as they cursed Jenna with all the bad words they could think of.

When CJ arrived, he came baring games, junk food and alcohol. "This is going to end badly," I said, groaning as Cat came bounding out of the living room to tease CJ or hug him; it's pretty much the same thing. Cat and CJ gushed about how great the other looked and started chatting about what they'd been up to since they last saw each other, and I kind of realised then that there was no chance of any brainstorming or gaming while Cat was around. Her bruises had almost healed, and I was pretty sure she was dying to get in front of a camera, so I asked Kate and Sasha to set up a photo shoot to occupy my darling sister. She'd only end up hurting CJ anyway, she didn't stay with anyone long enough to see out a year.

Eventually, the girls were set for their shoot. Cat happened to have a bunch of photography equipment in her safe car any way, god knows why, and they wandered off to find good lighting and decent clothes that would match Sasha's eccentric and arty make-up styles.

"Why did you make them leave?" CJ asked, looking lost in his boy band-ish looks.

"Because we need to deal with Jenna. You've known her the longest and I know her the best, we've got to be able to come up with something between us, right?" he nodded and shoved a game into the PS4. "You're so graceful," I commented, causing him to flip me off.

CJ and I were mind-blank. No plan seemed fool-proof and every plan seemed like it would get me and Sasha into an even worse situation. We knew we couldn't back Jenna into a corner. That would just cause her to act on her words faster and more viciously. Trying to reason had only fuelled her need to ruin us and I was starting to feel the strain of the threat.

I wanted to save Sasha from this threat that was looming over her head. She'd moved here to escape someone, and now she was being threatened by her lecturer, a person she was supposed to be able to trust. No wonder the poor girl was anxious. She had no idea why life kept throwing these things in her face and no one had an answer for her. I was starting to realise that the way I felt about Sasha wasn't just any old crushing romance. At first, I'd felt like I'd needed her presence, and when I had that, I needed her company, and eventually, it had led to this; Needing to protect her. I wasn't in liking with this girl, I was in love with her, and I knew I had to do something to stop Jenna, even if it meant I had to make some threats of my own.

The next day, CJ and I went to work and Kate and Sasha headed off to college. Sasha told me she didn't have a lesson with Jenna that day, so as long as she avoided the general direction of her classroom, she should be fine. I stood at the front of my class, listening to the students' debate over Romeo's true intentions and Juliet's naivety, hearing well-formed and thought out opinions. I was thinking about how ironic it was that I'd chosen to teach these people about the star crossed lovers, and Shakespeare's hidden meanings, way back at the beginning of the summer, just over a month before I even knew of Sasha's existence. It seemed now that my past self had known I'd find myself in a spot of trouble, and wanted to remind me that it's probably never going to be as bad as the fate of Romeo and Juliet.

I felt nervous as I finished my last class of the day. I didn't particularly want to see Jenna on her home turf, or at least the hotel she was staying in, but I knew there was no way I could get her to meet me on neutral ground, so this was the only way I could do this. I didn't tell Sasha I was going, and because I wouldn't be seeing her tonight, I felt guilty about it. I just didn't want to alarm her or make her even more worried unnecessarily.

Jenna's hotel was fancy. It was one hundred percent stepford (as Sasha would say) in its appearance, and I was pretty sure only the richest of people could stay here. I asked the front desk to find out if I could go up to Jenna, and was not at all surprised when she told them I could. She was going to try to sink her claws into me, but I was fully prepared this time.

"Hello Nicholas," she said quietly as I entered her room. It was far too tidy and made me feel ever so slightly on edge. I was acting as if it didn't though.

"Jenna, I came to talk about your sick behaviour towards my girlfriend, one of your students, I might add. I'm not here to exchange pleasantries." My voice stayed steady and strong, and I was glad of it.

"I thought as much, so what is it you have to say to me?" She strolled over to her bed and sat on the edge. I think she was trying to pull seductive faces, but she just looked like she was having some kind of facial issue.

"You threatened your student, and the way I see it, I don't think your managers would be very happy to hear about it, would they?" Her eyes widened and I kept my smug smile to a minimum.

"If you want to keep this little incident away from your employers' eyes and ears, I'd seriously suggest backing the hell off. Are we clear?" Jenna nodded, standing up suddenly and walking over to me.

Her face was inches from mine when she spoke in a low voice; "You know it won't last between you and that god awful girl, don't you? She's too compulsive and too rebellious for a stick in the mud like you. She'll want to move in with you even more than I did, and you'll be trapped again. You'll lose her, and you'll come crawling back to me. I'll be waiting baby, I promise," she smiled slyly and tried to caress my face. I caught her wrist and held it away from me.

"You're wrong," I growled through clenched teeth before dropping her wrist and leaving.

# CHAPTER EIGHT
*Sasha*

Nick phoned to tell me that he'd sorted things with Jenna Green. I'd never felt so relieved in my life. I actually felt more relieved than when my parents had told me I'd be moving hundreds of miles away from the stalker formerly known as Jase. I asked Nick what he'd said but he told me it wasn't important, and that all that really mattered was that we could be together without any pathetic interferences. My nagging anxiety lifted, the feeling of constant panic drifted away and eventually, I was left with a blissful feeling of calm as we talked about our days and joked on the phone. This was what it was supposed to be like. Fun, happy, and unencumbered by jealous women who acted like they were trustworthy people.

I went to sleep feeling refreshed and excited. Tomorrow was a new day and I felt as if nothing could touch me. I was in a new relationship, a real one with a decent, caring guy who seemed to want to do anything to protect me, my home life was a good as it always had been and my best friend and I were becoming incredibly close friends with an international super model, what could be better? I couldn't think of anything.

I groaned when my alarm went off. I may have gone to sleep happy, but no amount of sleep ever seemed to be enough to make me feel fully rested. I showered, got ready, and left my hair to dry naturally on the car ride to campus. I picked up Kate on the way and we discussed what we imagined Nick might have said to Green to make her back off. It must've been something powerful; I just hoped she hadn't been too upset about losing. She may be a hateful mess of a woman, but no one deserved to be unhappy, even her. Even with my moral reasoning, we were both excited to see her face when we rocked up all sunshine and smiles in class, although I promised myself I'd try not to be smug.

"Good morning everyone," Green said as she adjusted her brown flowing skirt and white blouse. She looked far older in that get up than she was, and it definitely wasn't her usual style. I started to get the feeling that she was up to something. A few people muttered a 'hi,' or 'hello,' back, but mainly we just sat at our desks. Most of the lesson went by like any other, and I started to relax thinking it was really over, and Miss Green had just decided to change her style to something a little less preppy, but eventually, it was time for her to ask questions, and then she really came down on me. She would ask a question, pick on me, and if I was right, which I most often was, she would pass me off as a know it all, attracting dirty glares and judging looks from my peers. When I was wrong, well, she turned it into an excuse to exploit me and use me as an example of everything that was wrong in the literary world. Eventually class ended, and I felt as if I'd been mentally slapped, kicked and punched in the brain. I thought about staying behind and giving the woman a piece of my mind, but I didn't want to fuel her fire any more than it already had been.

I didn't tell Nick about the ordeal. I acted like everything was fine and even told him that Jenna had been positively pleasant. I don't know why I lied, but a feeling in my gut told me that telling him what had really happened would just make things worse, and besides, he didn't need that stress when he had his own job and students to worry about.

The next few days worked in the same way. Miss Green would humiliate me in class and I would take it because I knew better than to rise to a bully. Kate kept telling me that I needed to tell Nick, but worrying him just wasn't something that I wanted to do, especially when it might fuel the hate fire.

Things came to a real head the day the Jane Eyre papers were handed back. I stared down at the document in front of me, twelve pages shorter than it had been when I handed it in, with an enormous, glaring red 'U' at the very top of the front page. My eyes stung with angry tears and my fists balled as I stood up for too quickly to be considered normal behaviour. "What the hell is this?" I shouted in disgust.

"That's your paper dear. Do sit down, you shouldn't make a scene over a bad grade," Green tutted.

"Are you freaking serious? You hateful, disgusting little bitch! Is this any way to treat a student?!" I yelled in disbelief. I knew I was making a fool of myself. Jenna had seen to it that I would, trashing my essay and writing snide comments in bold red pen all over the four pages that were actually left of my essay.

"Excuse me, Miss Santiago, but if you don't calm down, I will have to call for campus security to remove you from the building," she said, smiling sarcastically.

"Where is the rest of my essay?" I asked.

"Why, whatever do you mean? It's all there."

"I distinctly remember handing in a sixteen page essay on the underlying meaning of the text, In fact, I'm pretty sure everyone else here can remember me handing it in too because half of these people asked me why I'd written so much when they'd only written six or seven pages." I looked around me, pleading for back up with my eyes, but everyone in that class knew better than to go against a teacher, everyone except Kate. "She's right, Jenna. Do you mind if I call you that? Of course you don't. This is college, right? I was there when Sasha handed in that essay. I was there when she printed it off. I love how you've not even tried to disguise the fact that you've re-stapled this damn thing, you god awful woman. Give this girl the grade she deserves before I make your life a living hell." Kate put a hand on her hip and I looked at her in disbelief. She'd just jeopardised herself for me. No one had ever done that before. I felt the strong urge to cry and hug my best friend in thanks, but right now I needed to stand my ground.

"I'm very sorry girls, but you're going to have to leave my classroom. I'll be seeing you both for a meeting with the head of department to discuss your childish and foolish behaviour today. You will receive an email and a letter in the upcoming days giving you a time, place and date for your disciplinary hearing. Enjoy the rest of your day, I'll send a message to your other teachers to let them know you won't be in their lessons. Goodbye." Jenna smiled wickedly and waggled her fingers in our general direction like she'd done many times in the past couple of weeks. I was suddenly feeling as if I wasn't going to win this battle, so after I dropped Kate home, I headed to the East campus to see Nick.

The lady at reception told me he was teaching a class, but I'd be welcome to stick around until the end. I asked her if CJ was around, and luckily for me, he was. The woman handed me a yellow visitors pass and told me exactly how to get to CJ's classroom. Ironically, it was right beside Nick's, and the glass walls that separated the rooms caused Nick to see me, and excuse himself from his class to come and see me in CJ's room. "What's up?" he asked; worry drawing his eyebrows closer together.

"Nothing, it's fine. I'll tell you when you're finished teaching. I just need to talk to you about something," I tried to soothe. It was much harder when I couldn't reach up and scratch the side of his head like he liked, but he took my words with him back to his classroom and glanced at me occasionally while he carried on his lecture. CJ asked me what was up, but I told him I really couldn't tell him until Nick knew, so we sat talking casually until Nick's class was over. As soon as the last student left, CJ and I practically ran into Nick's room and locked the door behind us. "Don't get upset," I began, causing Nick's gorgeous brown eyes to widen in alarm. CJ grinned, "This will be good." I glared in CJ's general direction.

"I didn't tell you this, because I didn't want to worry you. I thought it would pass if I ignored it, but it hasn't." I paused, leaving just enough time for Nick to tell me to continue. "Green - Jenna, has been messing with me in class. Almost like a secretive and superior kind of bullying. I was handling it fine, until today. She handed me my Jane Eyre essay back, you know the one I was so excited about and proud of? Well, she handed back four pages, graded 'U'," Nick grimaced and began to pace while CJ cursed softly under his breath. "I flipped out, and she acted as if I was just a sore loser, pissed over a rough grade. She planned the whole thing because when Kate stood up for me, she made us both leave. We have to go to a disciplinary hearing to discuss the 'next steps.' Nick, I don't know what to do. If the head of department decides that Green is in the right, well, I'm done for. That was my penultimate essay, but a 'U'? Well, that cancels out every one of my previous Lit grades. I'll fail," I breathed out a shaky breath and looked up at the man I'd somehow fallen in love with in such a short space of time. He closed the short distance between us and wrapped his arms around my shoulders. He stroked my hair without speaking and eventually stepped away from me, sliding his hand down my arm and interlocking our fingers when he got to the end. The gesture was comforting and electrifying, even in this disastrous situation.

"Do you know when your disciplinary hearing is?" he asked. I shook my head. "Okay, you need to re-print that essay and take it with you to the meeting. Have a look at your computer and see if you can access your print history, then take a screenshot of the number of pages printed when you first handed in your essay. Try your best to catch Jenna out, make her feel cornered, if you can, in front of the authority, but subtly. I'll try to find out what the course of action for something like this is, and we'll deal with whatever happens together, okay?" I nodded again and he sighed.

"Who knew kissing someone in a club could bring so much hassle?" CJ muttered, making Nick and I both laugh.

"I should go," I admitted. "You have classes to teach and I have parents to explain a disciplinary to. I'll catch you later," I sighed, standing on the tips of my toes to press my lips longingly to his. It felt like forever since I'd last kissed him.

"Come over tomorrow?" he asked, and I agreed.

Neither of my parents were in when I got home, so I went upstairs to change and print off my essay again. I double checked it for spelling errors and misplaced punctuation before saving it, and finally sending it to the printer. I checked Facebook to see that Kate had already posted a strongly worded status full of expletives and a number of new nicknames for our lecturer. Once the essay had finished printing, I went downstairs and cooked up a kick ass Spaghetti Bolognese for my parents and a chicken carbonara for myself. That should soften the blow a little.

Telling my parents was far easier than I expected. They knew I wasn't a bad student, and I'd never had an outburst like this in class in all the years I'd been in education. I told them my teacher had been 'picking' on me, hating the sound of the word as it left my mouth, and they assured me they'd accompany me to my meeting and make sure I was treated fairly. I tried to tell them it was fine but they wouldn't listen.

The email for the disciplinary came around all too quickly, and the event even quicker. I dressed as smartly as I could, wearing black skinny jeans and a white blouse with a black cardigan, and my white converse. I tied my hair back and hoped I looked okay. My parents drove which left me feeling queasy and unsettled in the back. Driving always helped calm me down; it made me feel relaxed and preoccupied with staying alert on the road. I text Nick, who wished me luck and told me to call him when I knew what was going on. I agreed and wished this day would just be over and done with.

Stepping into the small, claustrophobic office was nerve wracking, but stepping in to see Jenna and the head of department already waiting made me feel like I was about to hurl. I felt a panic attack arising and I knew this was not the time for one of those. I tried to keep my breathing steady and confined the panic to a small corner of my brain, taking a seat beside my parents and trying my best to listen to what the head of department was describing as 'common procedure.'

"Now I understand you were unhappy with the grade Miss Green gave you Sasha, is that correct?" he asked. I nodded, thinking about my words before I said them.

"Yes, sir. She gave me a 'U' for my paper, but she only handed me back four pages. I thought it must have been a mistake, considering I handed in a sixteen page essay that I had spent weeks on. I have proof of the printing and a copy of the original essay here." I handed over the papers and I caught a small moment of uncertainty in Jenna's eyes but she soon covered that. "Anyway, I asked Miss Green what was going on. She tried to convince me, and the class, that I'd handed in four pages when witnesses saw me handing in much more than that. Another member of the class stood up for me and pointed out that the work had been re-stapled, and then we were both sent away and given disciplinaries. You have my new copy but I do have the re-stapled essay with me too, if you would like to see it," I breathed out and felt a little relieved when I saw Jenna's composure waver again, but her face hardened just as quickly as it had flickered worry, and she bit back like an untrained Rottweiler.

"You're full of lies. I'm sure the rest of your class would be ashamed at how easily you can spin such a web. Trying to pin this monstrous behaviour on your teacher." I snorted, causing the head of department to frown at me.

"Miss Santiago, it is clear that Miss Green and yourself have some unresolved issues, so if you would like to give me your full essay, I will have another lecturer mark it and get it back to you as soon as possible. In the meantime, I expect you to behave pleasantly towards Miss Green, and keep yourself out of trouble in her lessons," he smiled, acting as if he'd just solved the world's most difficult equation and gestured for my parents and myself to leave. Just as I was about to close the door behind me, I saw Jenna's mouth curve into a smile. She waggled her fingers at me again and I knew this was only going to get worse. I tried to breathe around the lump in my throat but all in all, I felt terrified.

When I got home, I text Kate the spark notes version of what had happened and then drove myself to Nick's. When I got there, Cat was getting ready to go out somewhere and Nick was sitting at his kitchen table in a pair of grey boxers and a light blue t-shirt. He looked absolutely adorable in his sleepy state and when he smiled at the sight of me, I felt a wave of calm wash over me. I dropped my bag in the hallway and rushed over to throw my arms around his neck. He pulled me onto his lap and stroked my hair soothingly whilst rubbing large circles into my back. "What happened?" he asked, shifting so he could see my face properly. I told him everything and felt so bad as I watched sadness take over his face, washing away the adorable sleepiness and leaving worry in its place.

"These people are so oblivious to the truth," he muttered angrily.

"At least I'm not going to fail. I'm so sorry about this Nick. You don't deserve it, not after breaking up with her. I wonder if we did the right thing, meeting up after the kiss in the club. I wonder if this is fate's way of telling us that we're not meant to be together," I admitted, finally releasing the heart breaking thoughts that had clouded my mind far too much for the beginning of a relationship. Nick frowned.

"These obstacles are just testing us Sash, they're preparing us for what could make or break us down the line. We met by coincidence, and we didn't know where life was going to lead us. These things that keep getting in the way are just fate's way of making sure we really are compatible and can work together. I can't write us off Sash, please don't make me write us off." His eyes were pleading and I knew he was right. I kissed him roughly, finally giving in to the need to feel human, and real. We fought for dominance, our tongues dancing in the war, mine finally giving in to the passion of his. I'd never been kissed quite like that, quite so thoroughly, but I liked it, and I'd needed it. I pulled away.

"You're right. I'm sorry," I whispered, letting a small smile creep onto my face before closing the distance between our lips once more.

# CHAPTER NINE

*Nick*

Sasha was still being bullied by Jenna in classes, but she was handling it as well as she could. I would never have been able to handle it that easily and she did it with such grace, too. We didn't see each other a lot over the next couple of weeks because our schedules were messy but when we did see each other, we made the most of it. We didn't talk about Jenna and made sure we were focusing on the here and now. It was working well. I was falling more in love with her every day and it suited me just fine. Everything was starting to take shape, and then Jenna threw another curveball.

There was a knock at my door; I looked at my watch, thinking that it wasn't like Sasha to be an hour early without texting first. It's not like I minded, it was just peculiar. When I opened the door, it wasn't Sasha standing before me. It was my mother. My entire body froze, my blood ran cold and I knew that Jenna had been involved in this. "What are you doing here?" I asked, trying not to sound as weak as I felt.

"I heard you'd gotten yourself into a *situation*," she sneered, pushing past me and throwing her long fur coat over the banister. Everything in me was screaming. This woman wasn't supposed to be here. I asked her to stay out of my life and she should have respected that. She made me feel sick and nervous. I never knew what she was going to do to me.

“Oh, and who told you that? It’s a lie.”

“That lovely girlfriend of yours, Jenna or at least your ex-girlfriend I hear now.”

“What did she say?”

“She told me that you have been fooling around with a girl who is highly unsuitable for you.”

“Unsuitable? How the hell would *she* know who’s suitable for me?” I tried to sound calm, keeping as far away from my mother as possible.

“She was suitable for you, this new young woman isn’t, and it’s as simple as that. How do you expect to have a successful life when you’re running around with a low-life college student with a sales assistant’s job in a book shop?” The woman had always reminded me of Cruella De Vil, but somehow today even more so.

“How do you even know where she works?” This woman was ridiculous. I think a sheen of sweat was starting to form over my forehead and my head was getting foggy. This flat was mine, it was my escape, and now she was filling it with bad memories.

"You know I have my ways. Don't be naïve Nicholas. Now, get your mother a drink."

"You don't need a drink. Shouldn't you be getting back?" I didn't want her to be here when Sasha arrived.

"Get your mother a drink and stop your complaining. You're acting like a child Nicholas. A child running around with other childish people. I hear you're harbouring your sister, letting her run away from her problems instead of facing them just like you do."

"Do not bring Cat into this. We wouldn't need to run away from our problems if we didn't have a wreck of a mother like you. You drove dad away, and then you drove us away with your sick behaviour and drinking. I don't know why Jenna called you and I don't know why you bothered coming here, but my life is none of your god damn business and you need to leave." I regretted my words straight away. My mother stood up and with a movement quicker than a viper, she slapped me. I suddenly felt like a kid again. I remembered the fear that consumed me as soon as my mother would get home from work, the overwhelming desire to crawl out of my own skin and life and the nights I spent quivering under my quilt, waiting for my parents' arguing to stop, wondering if she'd come into my room and beat her frustration out on me like she so often did. The memories of seeing my dad the morning after one of their arguments with a black eye or scratches down his arms, and after he left, fighting with my mother and being the one to receive even more of those bruises and marks, they all came back to me.

I stepped away from the tyrant that stood in front of me, resisting the urge to bring my hand to my cheek to assess the damage, knowing the satisfaction of knowing I was in pain would only spur her on. I shouldn't have angered her. I know what you're thinking, 'why don't you fight back, Nick? Why don't you defend yourself?' Well, the answer is simple; no matter how bad it got, no matter how much it hurt, I was taught never to hit a woman, and so I'd done exactly what my dad had done. I'd gotten out, and Cat had done it too. We left that disgusting woman to her own devices and we made it on our own, but now Jenna has brought her into my flat, into my life and into my head. My mother took a step closer to me, speaking in a low voice. "Don't you dare raise your voice to me," she raised her hand again and I felt relief and then terror as the doorbell rang. I couldn't let Sasha in, but I could get myself away from my mother if I went and told her to leave. I walked around my mother, keeping as much distance as I could. It wasn't enough. "Don't answer that door," she warned as she grabbed my arm. I felt the sting of her painted red nails dig into my skin, and then I felt the warmth of the blood flow from the broken skin as I ripped myself away from her. I rushed to the front door, and stepped out of it, closing it behind me so that Sasha knew something was up. Usually, I'd just open the door and head straight to whatever room we were hanging out in at the time.

"What's up?" she asked me, before seeing the handprint on my cheek and blood on my arm. Concern and worry clouded her face. "Nick, you're bleeding, what the hell is going on? Did Jenna do this?" she asked, furiously, trying to push past me into the flat.

"No. Sash, look, you need to go. It's not Jenna. There's stuff I haven't told you, about my family. I can't get into it now but please, you need to leave before it's too late," I pleaded, trying to keep my voice down so that my mother wouldn't hear. I was too late though. Before Sasha could walk away, my mother was opening the door behind me. I turned around, positioning myself in front of Sasha, and reached behind me to take her hand.

"Hello dear, I'm Nicholas' mother, who might you be?" Trust my mother to play it so politely on the street, making me look crazy.

Sasha's fingers tightened around mine reassuringly. "I'm Sasha Santiago, Nick's girlfriend." She held the hand I wasn't holding out towards my mother, stepping forward. God this girl was brave. She didn't know what she was getting herself into, though. My mother took her hand, I saw her knuckles turn white for a second or two before she let go, leaving Sasha to flex her fingers while my mother invited her into *my* home.

At first, things went fine. My mother was surprisingly polite while Sasha cleaned the gouges on my arm with salt water and held ice to my face, and Sasha didn't ask questions, though I knew she wanted to. It was when we were done with the first aid that things went downhill. I already felt uncomfortable with Sasha being in such close quarters with my mother. Who knew what kind of crazy shit that woman would pull on my girlfriend? When she started questioning her like she was a criminal, I just wanted to bury myself. My mother was making Sasha feel uncomfortable, I could see it, but neither of them backed down. It was like Sasha had an answer for everything, but my mother kept thinking up more questions. I was feeling boxed in, like I was standing in a sauna with no door. I knew how compulsive Sasha could be, and I didn't want her to piss my mother off. I never imagined it would go the other way around. My mother shifted her attention to me with no warning at all. "What on earth do you see in this foolish child?" she asked me. I blinked, no words formed in my brain, I was literally speechless.

"Excuse me?" Sasha asked. I could hear the anger in her voice. Since Jenna had been messing with her, she'd become a lot feistier.

"You heard, or are you deaf as well as stupid now? You know you're not good enough for my son. You know you're not old enough for him and you definitely know you're not smart enough for him or else why would you be spending so much time trying so desperately to hold on? Any self-respecting woman would have given up and let the right woman win, but you're just hanging in there like a little leech, hoping that this wreck of a young man won't realise how wrong you are for him until it's far too late," she sniffed and stood up, but Sasha wasn't backing down. I wished she would back down.

"Clearly you have some issues, lady. No wonder Nick and Cat don't talk about their family when they have Cruella for a mother. Christ woman, can't you see how wrong your mind is? Can't you see that drawing blood from your own son's arm is sick and twisted and disgusting? It is abuse, and clearly this isn't the first time you've done it," Sasha spat. My mother lunged then, clawing out for Sasha with the most grotesque expression on her face. Her eyes were bulging, her skin was turning red and I knew something had to be done before someone got seriously hurt. I'd never stood up to my mother before. I'd never felt strong enough to physically force her to leave, but in that second, when I saw how desperately she wanted to hurt Sasha, I knew there was only one thing I could do. I grabbed my mother's shoulders harshly and steered her towards the door. I don't know why I'd never done it before; it seemed so easy now. I threw her out of my house and slammed the door. A few seconds later shock set in and I sank to the floor just in front of my door. Sasha rushed over and tried to calm me down but my head was a blur. I couldn't think, I couldn't see, I just felt scared. I felt like a kid again, but this time I felt like a kid who needed to protect someone else too. I dropped my head into my hands and just let the hurt take over. Sasha wrapped her arms around me, enveloping me in this warm, loving embrace that I didn't think I'd ever get the chance to feel. She rocked me back and forth until I could finally breathe and think again, and then she made me a cup of coffee and we sat at the kitchen table discussing what had happened.

We stayed up late that night. I explained absolutely everything to Sasha, from my mum abusing my dad, to him leaving and her getting custody of me and Cat. I also mentioned us finally leaving and coming to Ravens End for university, and Cat getting discovered by some modelling agent at a school fashion show, then I moved on to meeting CJ and Jenna, and I even still looked upon our memories as good ones. We finally got to details of the break up, how it had all started over her wanting to move in and how I'd known right then that our relationship was wrong. Sasha didn't judge me though. She didn't storm out or ask if I was going to do the same to her down the line. She just listened and understood, and eventually, she kissed me goodnight: softly, sweetly and went home.

I shouldn't have answered my door at three o'clock in the morning. I should've stayed in bed and pretended I was asleep, but I was stupid, and I did it anyway. Part of me hoped my mother would return one last time so I could tell her to stay out of all of our lives for good, but then I remembered even I wasn't that masochistic. I wasn't sure if the reality was better or worse.

Jenna was standing on my doorstep, a smile on her face and a bottle of expensive wine in her hand. I went to shut the door but she pushed past me before my reflexes could kick in. She wandered straight through to the kitchen and took two wine glasses from the cupboard. "What're you doing?" I asked. She just laughed and placed a glass in front of me.

"We're celebrating," she smiled. I looked at her blankly, and after a long, uncomfortable silence, she finally elaborated. "We're celebrating the fact that I've finally found the formula to winning. Oh Nick, don't frown at me like that, you know it would come to this. You've been intent on sabotaging all of my plans, you and Sasha both. You've kept on with your dirty little secret through all that I've done to try and make you both see that it's wrong. I've only got your best interests at heart darling. Anyway, in a few hours, something very, very interesting is going to happen, and you're going to be left Sasha-less. I know you're probably thinking there's no way I could win after everything you've been through so far, but you're mistaken. I'll text you my plan in due course; I'd stay by your phone if I were you." She stood up and left without another word. I tried to chase after her but my thoughts were slow and unformed in my sleepy state. My head pounded and I knew I needed to go back to sleep again, maybe the weird incident was just a dream, after all.

It wasn't a dream. At seven AM, I got a text from Jenna.

'You'll be interested to know that these photos are currently sitting in an anonymous envelope on Sasha Santiago's welcome mat.'

Attached to the text were several pictures of me and Sasha when we'd been saying hello in my classroom what felt like months ago, but was only really weeks.

'How does this affect any one? A girl is allowed to kiss her boyfriend,' I replied, receiving a phone call not even a minute after.

"It's amazing what those photos look like when given a story without context. That envelope doesn't just contain pictures. It also contains a letter from a concerned friend, wanting the best for both parties," Jenna cackled before putting the phone down. I don't think I've ever moved so fast in my life. I got washed and dressed within a matter of minutes, trying Sasha's phone the whole time. I was hoping it would magically turn itself on in the two seconds it took me to redial. I then phoned Kate, asking her for Sasha's address. Luckily she had her phone on. She asked me what was up, and when I told her, she told me she'd meet me at Sasha's.

It took me far too long to get there. My satnav was wrong and I was running out of time. Kate met me at the end of the driveway and we rushed up together, Kate trying Sasha's phone even more obsessively than I had. Finally, she rang the doorbell. A woman with coppery coloured hair and a pink pastel dressing gown opened the door. When she saw me, she went a pale shade of white and told me I had better come in. Kate and I followed the woman through the living room to another room that leads off from it, directly opposite to the front door to the kitchen. Sasha was sat in her frog shorts and my sweatshirt on a barstool at what I assumed was a breakfast bar. A tall, thin man with jet black hair stood opposite her looking furious and also a little sad.

"What are you doing here young man?" he asked, not pausing for a response. "Haven't you done enough?"

The woman in the pastel dressing gown went to stand behind her husband, leaving me and Kate standing awkwardly in the middle of the room. I took a step towards Sasha, but her father barked at me to stay where I was. I held my hands up in a surrendering gesture and to explain. "Mr. and Mrs. Santiago, the words in that letter are a lie. I can tell you for a fact because the woman who wrote that letter is my ex-girlfriend. She told me she was going to try to jeopardise mine and Sasha's relationship by getting you involved, but clearly, I'm too late. I am not Sasha's teacher. I have never taught her, and I never will. I teach at the East College which is not affiliated with the South in any way, shape or form. Those photos, though they may look very convincing, are deceiving, and were taken when Sasha came to visit me during my lunch hour. Please don't believe the lies in that envelope." It was all I could say, and I knew, just looking at the livid man, that it wasn't enough.

"You expect me to believe you when there is evidence sitting right in front of me that suggests the opposite to what you are saying? You really do have some nerve." He turned to Sasha, "I thought you were smarter than this, Frog, after everything you went through with that other boy, after having to move your entire life here, I thought you would be more careful," he sighed. I saw Sasha flinch; her hands clenched her knees like they did when she panicked, and she was clearly entirely uncomfortable. She looked at me fleetingly and then looked back at her dad.

"Nick isn't lying, Dad. He's not my teacher, and those photos are manipulated and deceitful. He's not the bad guy here. I know you're not going to listen, but he's not." She stood up, looking from her parents, to Kate, to me. She walked over, taking one of my hands in both of hers and looked straight into my eyes, as if she was boring her deepest thoughts into my soul. She lifted her right hand to caress the side of my face, and then moved it into my hair and scratched softly. "I'm sorry," she whispered, before walking straight out of the front door and driving off in her car. I was glued to the spot, completely lifeless and full of shock. That gesture felt like goodbye.

# CHAPTER TEN
## *Sasha*

I was driving around barefoot and in my pyjamas. My feet felt raw and I had my heater on cold because I felt as if my head was about to explode. I was feeling as if the entire world was crashing down around me. I don't know what had made me leave like that, but I had to get out. I knew my parents weren't going to budge on the matter of me and Nick, and I didn't want to give him time to realise what I was about to do. I didn't kiss him goodbye. I couldn't face it; I couldn't put either of us through the pain of it. Tears started to cloud my vision and I had to pull into a dingy looking café on the side of the road. I had no idea where I was, or where I was going, but I definitely needed to calm myself down and stop crying before I drove any further. Sobs wrenched from my gut and my hands shook uncontrollably. I felt as if my heart had been ripped from my chest in one desperate act to keep it with Nick. He'd had it since the moment we'd met, and when I left him standing in my kitchen, I left it with him. But I couldn't take it anymore. Jenna had won. If she hadn't won this, she would have found something else that weakened us, and she would've carried on until neither of us had anything left to give. I knew deep down she would've sucked all of the energy and life from our relationship, and left us with nothing but the shell of an epic love.

I left Nick standing with my family and Kate because it was better to leave him knowing that we had something special, and real, than to have everything we loved about one another stripped away, week by week until we were both soulless, empty human beings with no hearts left to love with. I was already kicking myself, sitting in that freezing cold car, barely clothed with one last piece of Nick still wrapped around me, but I couldn't go back on my decision. Nick would love again. He was gorgeous, intelligent, funny, and kind, and it wouldn't take long for a beautiful woman his own age to snap him up and give him the kind of love he needed, without interference from Jenna and without threats from his mother.

Nick would get over me, and us, because he was strong and amazing. He'd gotten through so much and he didn't need me ruining his life. I can see it now, sitting here, frozen and alone in a deserted car park next to a café that had definitely seen better days. I was trouble for him from the start. This town never would have let him be with a girl like me for long. I was wrong to this town. The girl that moved and made out with a guy eight years older than her in a club built for the rebellious. I could have cost Nick everything he'd built for himself, and really we should be thanking Jenna for making us realise that, right?

I wasn't kidding anyone. Not even myself. I didn't want Nick to find a beautiful woman that couldn't get the right sugar to coffee ratio. I didn't want him falling in love with some illiterate slut bag in a bar or even one of Cat's model friends. I didn't want him with another lecturer, or a writer, or any other kind of girl. I didn't want him with anyone but me. I wanted to go back and apologise for leaving, I wanted to tell him I'd made a mistake saying goodbye and that Jenna had just gotten to me, but I remembered my parents' faces. How disappointed they were in me. They didn't care how old he was, they didn't even care that I'd kissed him in a club, but they thought he was my teacher, they thought he was wrong, and they believed him a liar and that was enough for them to see their only child as damaged, rightly or wrongly. I couldn't go back to him now. I couldn't rip myself away from him only to crawl back to him. I couldn't mess with his head, not like Jenna had. I was letting him go for the right reasons, I convinced myself. I had to let him go.

I couldn't calm myself down, and eventually, I had to call Kate. She got her dad to bring her to the café, and then made me switch from the driver's side to the passenger side. She got into the car and started the engine, turning on the heat and buckling her seat belt. "Why did you do that?" she asked softly.

"I can't be the one to ruin his life," I choked, wiping tears furiously from my eyes only to have them replaced by more.

"Sash, you are his life, he's devastated," she reasoned.

"He will get over me. He has to."

"Sash you're a state but you need to listen to me. He doesn't want to get over you, he just wants you. He doesn't care about Jenna. He doesn't care what your parents think or what they believe, he told them that himself, I was there. He just wants you. When you walked out of that door he looked like you'd taken his heart with you. Those devastatingly gorgeous brown eyes that you talk about so much filled with tears, that's not a guy that's better off without you babe, that's a guy that needs you to complete him." She looked over at me and smiled, reassuringly.

"Kate, I know you're trying to help but it's over. I can't let him love me when I'm ruining his life." I turned away from her, closing my eyes while I leant my head against the cool window. Tears were still flowing freely and sobs wrenched themselves from my chest intermittently, but I didn't want to talk anymore.

When Kate parked my car in my driveway, she offered to come in and spend some time with me but I declined. I went straight to my room and threw myself into bed. My phone buzzed constantly, and eventually I turned it off, throwing it into my desk draw where it couldn't bother me anymore. My parents tried to talk to me throughout the day but I didn't respond. I knew this wasn't their fault, but I wasn't up to talking right now. Eventually my sobs died down and I fell asleep, taking the hurt of the day and leaving it floating about my room while my dreams took over.

*

I knew I was dreaming, the light was too bright, the grass too green, and the sun too hot for an autumn afternoon, but my mind wanted to take the hurt away, so it took me to a place I'd never been to before. There was a waterfall, surrounded by rocks that were covered in vines and little purple and yellow flowers. At the bottom of the waterfall was a little pool of clear blue, un-polluted water, and the beautiful little oasis was surrounded by woodland. The trees were gnarled and witchy looking, but not in a bad way. The whole place felt peaceful and beautiful. I breathed in, smelling floral scents and the rich waft of freshly watered earth, and eventually, the linen and woodsy smell of Nick. His arms wrapped around me from behind, his lips grazed my neck and he whispered to me. He told me he loved me, he asked me to never let him go, and I agreed. I told him I never wanted him to leave me. I told him I loved him too, and then he stepped back, glaring at me, not really focusing on me anymore. "I'm sorry," he said sharply and left. I tried to follow him through the forest but the dream wouldn't let me. I couldn't move at all, I just stood there, in this beautiful utopia, alone and scared, screaming for Nick when I knew he wasn't coming back. It started to rain, but the drops felt like icy knives piercing my skin over and over and over.

*

I woke up with a start. My skin felt too dry, my eyes too sore, and my head too foggy. I rubbed my temples and felt my entire body slump when the events of the day came back to me. My room was pitch black, the alarm clock on my bedside reading 2:47 AM. I sighed. I hadn't eaten since seven the morning before, and I knew I should feel hungry, but I just didn't. I got up to go to the bathroom and splashed my face with water. Tears started to pour again and I felt sick and lonely. I jumped in the shower, thinking the onslaught of scolding hot droplets would calm me down, but it only made things worse. I slid down the wall under the water, letting it drench me while I curled my knees up to my chest and cried. I needed Nick. I needed to be in his arms, but I couldn't be, if I could, I wouldn't even be in this position in the first place, and this all came down to Jenna. Suddenly I didn't want to mope. I didn't want to be up at 3a.m., crying in the shower, I wanted to have a life, I wanted to spend time with my boyfriend, but I couldn't, because, well, Jenna fucked it up, didn't she? She'd made it impossible for us to be together, and she'd made our lives hell. I stood up, washing the conditioner out of my hair and stepping out of the shower, wrapping my fluffy orange towel around me. There was nothing else I could do tonight, but I wanted revenge.

I woke up again at six. My hair was a mess of tangled waves that would hopefully look badass once I was finished with them. I got up and got washed quickly, before pulling on my favourite light blue, incredibly ripped skinny jeans and a loose grey vest top that really showed off my assets. I threw a black shirt over the top and then sat at my desk to do my hair and makeup. I brushed out the tangles and pulled all of my hair to one side, putting it into a fishtail plait and setting off the look with a diamante headband that reminded me of a tiara. I smoked out my eyes quickly, not really needing to spend long on them when I'd practiced the look for years, and added some pink red lip paint and strawberry lip gloss. My eyes were still a little red, and they stung like hell, but it only fuelled my fire. My white converse wasn't going to cut it today, I needed something that would give me some edge, like my black suede wedge boots with the studs on the heels. I called Kate, asking her if she could bring them when I picked her up, she told me she'd meant to give them back anyway, I laughed a little sarcastically and told her she could borrow them again after today.

Kate bought the shoes and I could've sworn they looked even better than they did when I bought them. She slung them in the back of the car and asked me what I was planning. I just smiled. When we got into town, we grabbed a Starbucks and headed straight to Jenna's lesson. I'd changed into the boots before we left the car, so I was all set to go ape shit. I know it was the worst idea, and I know it was wrong, but I was hurt, and quite frankly, all I needed right then was to be angry.

I sat in my usual seat in class, right in the centre, and then I waited. Jenna came into class around five minutes late. She was carrying a flask and a briefcase, like she was trying so hard to be this respectable role model or something. At least I knew her act was a lie. She didn't realise I was there for at least three minutes, but when she saw me sitting there, smiling, with the bags under my eyes expertly covered, her face dropped, her briefcase fell from her grip and her flask was slammed onto the table. My smile grew wider. My head was telling me that this was a bad idea, but my heart was telling me that I needed to get her back for what she'd done to me, and more importantly to Nick.

I didn't start straight away. I don't know why, but I kind of wanted to see what she had to say. I wanted to see if she had a remorseful bone in her body, but it turns out she didn't. Jenna started picking apart one of my very first essays in front of the entire class. I put my hand up, feeling myself going red as the entire class started to laugh at the adaptations she'd made to what I'd written.

“Yes Sasha?” she asked.

“Aren’t you supposed to keep your student’s work confidential or something?”

“Well, I only want to show the class how not to go wrong,” she smiled.

“I’m pretty sure the only way anyone in this room is going to achieve that is by ignoring you. Let’s be honest, it’s not like you’re stable.”

“Excuse me?” Her eyebrows rose and her mouth set into a hard line. I smiled. I wanted her to feel uncomfortable and I wanted her life under a microscope. I wanted her to know how she’d made me feel.

“I think you heard. I mean, let’s be honest, you’re not exactly a role model are you?”

“And what is that supposed to mean?”

“You really don’t want me to continue Jenna, trust me you don’t,” I warned.

“I don’t know. See, I really want to see what delusions you’ve cooked up for yourself. You’ve always had a good imagination Miss Santiago.”

“Okay, well let’s see...” I paused, leaning back in my seat and crossing my legs. “You tell your boyfriend you're moving in with him, and then insult his life when he says he's not ready for that. Then you see him with a new girl and take pictures just in case they might aid you in the future. Next, you make his new girlfriend's life absolute hell. You destroy her essays, you make fun of her and treat her like an absolute asshole, causing her to go off on one and get herself a disciplinary. From there, you call your ex boyfriend's abusive mother and try to get her to split the new couple up," I laughed bitterly, pausing to take in my classmates' faces. "Hang in there guys, we're not done yet. The last thing you did. The breaking point for that poor, poor couple, was to use those photos you took weeks ago, to fabricate yourself a nice little story about a student going out with her lecturer. You then wrote a heartfelt letter expressing your deepest concerns about their relationship to that poor girl's parents. But you lied, didn't you? He was never her lecturer, they'd never met before that night in the club, but you knew her parents wouldn't believe such a wild story: a crazy ex, out to destroy them. So you won. Well done Jenna, you won. Are you happy? Do you feel good about yourself? Well?" I stood up, staring her down before turning my back on the class and leaving.

I went and sat in my car, waiting for Kate to do whatever she was going to do, follow me or sit out the class, whatever. I swapped from my boots to my converse and then sat in the silence of my car. I slowly became aware of everything that had happened in the past 24 plus hours. I realised that I couldn't go to Nick's tonight to laugh and unwind. I couldn't kiss those perfect lips or feel those arms around me. I couldn't have Nick anymore. He wasn't mine and I wasn't his, no matter how wrong it felt to think that. My throat started to feel tight as I bit back tears. I balled my hands into fists, trying to fight the waves of depression that were threatening to take over my entire body. The waves of depression turned slowly into waves of anger and the rage I'd felt last night was coming slowly back to me. I got out of my car and slammed the door, clicking the lock button as I stormed furiously back into the building.

Jenna was trying to dig herself out of her hole when I re-entered the room, and Kate looked as if she was making notes on the whole thing. Everyone looked towards me as I threw the door open, but I barely registered their faces. I was seeing red and my fury was focused completely on Jenna. I felt my mouth set as I walked slowly towards Jenna. I raised my hand and bitch slapped her, soap style. Then I turned around and left again. I knew I was going to be in mounds of trouble, but I'd handed in my last essay already, there really wasn't anything keeping me there, and letting out my rage actually felt good for the first five minutes. Then guilt washed over me and I felt awful for stooping so low. Kate caught up with me at the car, gushing about how amazing I was for standing my ground and holding my own, but I just kept quiet, feeling wrong for sinking to Jenna's level.

# CHAPTER ELEVEN
*Nick*

Sasha's goodbye left me standing, shocked and broken in the middle of her kitchen. I started to defend myself, to try and prove that the letter was wrong, but her parents looked like they were about to shoot me. Luckily Kate had the sense to get me out of there when Sasha's father pointed at the door with a death glare on his face. She took my keys from me and drove me home, leaving me to my own devices while Cat drove her back to her own place.

I put my head in my hands as I thought things over. I was the happiest I'd ever been when I was with Sasha. She was so full of life, craziness and fun, and that was exactly what my life had been lacking. I'd lived with a fear of the unknown my whole life, but Sasha made the unknown exciting; she made me look forward to the future instead of dreading what was to come and fearing getting older. Sasha made me a better, happier version of myself and Jenna had destroyed it all in less than a day. I don't know what made her so revengeful. When we'd been together, she'd been sweet and kind, and a great girl, but we'd fallen out of love and it seemed as if she was still living in this dream world where we hadn't. I groaned, falling sideways onto my sofa and burying my face in the worn leather of the arm. I must've fallen asleep because I ended up waking up to the sound of voices trying to talk quietly. It was Cat and CJ. "So exactly how long has he been asleep?" CJ asked.

"Well, he was already asleep when I got home so I'm going to say anywhere between five and six hours. I don't think he's ever slept that long without getting up for something or the other," Cat replied. It was true, I'd never been one to sleep well.

"What happened?"

"Well, I got most of the story from Kate. There are still some parts I'm a little sketchy on, but Jenna has been messing with Nick for a while, which Kate told me you knew, and it all came to a head this morning when she sent pictures to Sasha's parents, claiming that Nick was her lecturer. He went to try and stop it from happening, but it was too late as her parents basically said there was no way they were continuing, and then Sasha drove off in her pyjamas. That poor girl must be heartbroken."

"Cat babes, Sasha has Kate, but right now, my best mate, your brother, is sleeping on his sofa in the middle of the day while he's supposed to be teaching. I think *he* might be heartbroken," Cat sighed and I really just wanted them to both stop talking.

I groaned and rolled over. "I'm fine guys," I muttered, sitting up and rubbing my temples as the morning came back to me. "I'm not going to fall apart." They both looked at me sympathetically. "I'm serious. I'm not going to fall apart, because I'm going to get her back." They cocked their heads, a mirror image of each other. "Seriously, I'm getting her back." I didn't know it until I said it, but it was true. I was going to do everything I possibly could to get her back, starting with sorting Jenna out. I stood up, feeling suddenly inspired to take hold of my life properly and do something about the shit that's gone on far too long. I grabbed my jacket and my keys, slamming the front door behind me as I headed to my car. I drove straight to Jenna's hotel, knowing I would probably regret whatever came next, but understanding her reasoning was the first step to making her leave us alone.

Jenna smiled wickedly when she saw me. That seemed to be the only smile she seemed to be able to manage recently. "What brings you here Nicholas?" she asked, wandering into her room as she scooped her blonde hair up into a ponytail.

"Why?" I asked simply.

"Whatever do you mean?"

"You know exactly what I mean. Why do you keep torturing me and Sasha? Why do you keep trying to split us up? Why can't you just let us be, build a bridge, get over it and move on?" Maybe that last part was a little harsh, but tough love and all that.

"Look, I know you don't understand why I'm doing this Nick, but it's for the best, it really is. You don't realise it now, but you still love me, and if you carry on with Sasha, you're just going to end up hurting her. You won't be able to handle hurting her Nick, I'm just protecting you both." She really believed it too. I shook my head.

"Jenna, please, you have to let this go. We're not meant to be together. We fell out of love a long time ago and if you were honest with yourself, you'd see it. We were on the rocks for months and your attempt to move in was the catalyst that tipped us over the edge. You need to let this go, because if you don't, you'll only end up bitter and alone, and you'll drag me down with you, apparently." I sounded so desperate and I was. Desperate to shake her out of her delusion.

"Why won't you just accept that we're meant to be together Nick? Why won't you admit that this was all just a game to make me jealous like I know it was?"

"Because it wasn't, and isn't Jenna. You're not winning this." I breathed out an exasperated sigh and got up to leave. "You need to let this go."

I felt so defeated when I got home. I knew I was setting myself up to fail but a small part of me still thought I'd succeed. I went to bed with a frown on my face and I woke up just the same. I got up, showered, dressed in a trance and by the time I actually even registered the fact that I was awake, I was already at work. My first class was studying Romeo and Juliet. After the first month went so well, I decided to extend it to all my classes. I once again realised how ironic it was that I'd chosen the play about the star crossed lovers only to find my own relationship taking its own little star crossed turn. I sighed audibly, causing a few of my students to look up and frown. "Okay guys, so what are your opinions on Nurse? Is she concerned for Juliet, or only interested in herself? That's your homework for this week. I want you to make notes and form opinions, and then we'll discuss them next week," I smiled, running a hand through the front of my hair as I went to sit behind my desk. As the last few students filed out, I heard some whisperings. "Did you hear about what happened over at the South College this morning?" A blonde gossip named Rayna asked her current boyfriend George.

"No, but I'm sure you'll tell me," he muttered sarcastically.

"No, you'll like this," she assured him. "A student went off at a lecturer. Apparently, the lecturer has been messing in her personal life, and the student slapped the woman! Elle said it was crazy; this chick just flipped out and started screaming at her lecturer, left the lesson, and then came back ten minutes later to slap her. Apparently, her best friend took notes when the..." they left the room, still talking, but I would bet any money that Kate was the one taking notes. This was too coincidental to not be about Sasha and Jenna. I had to find out what had happened. I called Kate, locking my classroom door to avoid any intrusions.

She answered on the third ring. "I wondered how long it would be before you got wind of the *situation*."

"What the hell happened?"

"Well, Sash picked me up this morning in a kind of badass mood. She asked me to give her wedge boots back so she could wear them to class, and when we got there, she just acted as if nothing was wrong. I mean, clearly there was, but you know Sash, she acts as if everything's okay when the apocalypse is happening, so her outburst was kind of surprising. I make her right though. Jenna's gotten away with way too much and she finally got a slap for it," She laughed.

"So it was really that simple? How is she?" I asked.

"She's not good. I'm not going to lie to you. She's acting as if everything's fine still but she's snappy and angry and she's completely ignoring her parents. Her dad asked her what happened today when we got back to hers and she literally acted as if he didn't exist. I've never seen her like that before; she's always been close to her parents. She might be a tough cookie but she needs you. That night at the club, it was like you awakened some sort of spark in her, it seemed as if she finally took a breath and relaxed, and now she's all tense again," she sighed.

"Kate I need to get her back."

"I agree, I'm taking her to Fivers tonight to try to chill her out a bit, you should come. Uh, I have to go, she's coming." She put the phone down and I was left to wonder what time I was supposed to turn up.

I decided to get to Fivers for seven, and I wished I'd gotten there earlier. I knew for a fact Sasha didn't drink, but she was sitting at the bar, slumped over with several shot glasses and a bottle of beer in front of her. Kate looked up at me the minute I entered the bar, her eyes pleading with me to help. Sasha was crying and muttering something about never getting it right. "Sash, come on, we need to get you home," I said, slipping an arm around her waist and hoisting her up so that Kate could support her other side.

"I've never seen her like this," she squeaked. Sasha looked up at me, bleary eyed and smiled. She might've been wasted but that smile was enough to assure me that she wasn't ready to give up on us.

"Nick," she whispered before passing out.

We took her back to mine and gave her coffee and several slices of toast to sober her up. By the time she was speaking in coherent sentences, she was too tired to hold her head up. I carried her to my room and left her to sleep it off in my bed, while I went to the kitchen to talk with Kate. "I thought she didn't drink?" I muttered a question in my voice.

"She doesn't, usually. She hates alcohol. Apparently tonight was a *special occasion,*" Kate sighed. "I'm going to head home. Let me know how she is in the morning?" I nodded, following her to the front door to see her out. I stood outside my bedroom door for far too long before deciding to crash in the bath with some spare blankets and pillows. The last thing Sasha needed was to wake up confused and disorientated next to me.

Sasha found me in the morning. She nudged me awake and I was pretty surprised to see that she was furious. "What the hell am I doing here?" she asked, half shouting.

"Do you not remember?"

"Would I be asking if I remembered, Nick? Christ."

"Fair point. Why are you mad?"

"Because we're broken up. We can't be together and I shouldn't be here." She sat on the edge of the tub and ran a hand through her hair. "I can't be here."

"You were drunk, I didn't think you'd want to explain that to your parents, so I brought you here to sober you up," I explained. She frowned, standing up suddenly.

"You can't save me now Nick, you're not my boyfriend. I need you to leave me alone because if you don't, this is all going to get worse. I need you to stay away," she paused, her lip quivering and hands shaking. "I need you to forget about me," she squeaked, voice cracking as tears filled her eyes. She rubbed them furiously, looking scared and lost. "I need you to drive me home, please, and then I need you to leave me be. I'm sorry but it has to be this way." I nodded, knowing my heart was in shock but not really feeling it. I was numb. I got out of my makeshift bed, brushed my teeth and grabbed my keys.

"Well then, let's go."

We stayed silent for the entire journey, she stared out the window and I focused on not losing my head while my entire body was screaming at me to do something, to stop this from happening, but I couldn't. Sasha wasn't going to let 'us' happen, so I'd have to think of another plan. I parked up around the corner from her house, per her request, and tried to stay silent as she began to get out of the car. At the last minute, I grabbed her wrist. She turned half way to look at me, her eyes questioning. "I love you," I whispered. She nodded, entwining her fingers with mine for a second before pulling away.

"I love you too." And then she was gone.

When I got home, I only had about twenty minutes to get ready and leave for work. It wasn't long enough. My body was sluggish and weak with the depression of knowing that what felt like the love of my life had just walked out of it. My shirt wasn't ironed, my tie was loose and I wore odd shoes, not paying the slightest bit of attention to how I must've looked. My students whispered and my colleagues frowned, probably wondering what the hell was wrong with me, but I knew what was wrong with me. I was incomplete.

I let my students write their essays throughout my classes and locked my door at break times. CJ tried to ask me what was wrong but I didn't feel like talking. I was spiralling and to be perfectly honest, I didn't care.

Home felt wrong. Cat's stuff was still scattered to the four winds, my music was still where it should be, my kitchen was the same as it had always been, but it was wrong. When Jenna had left, I'd felt relieved that she wasn't around anymore, but with Sasha gone, I felt empty. I wasn't even sad, I was just numb and cold and sick to my stomach with the constant lump in my throat. Heart break. I was nothing. My flat meant nothing, my music meant nothing, my books and my qualifications, all my achievements, they meant nothing at all because the one person I wanted to share them all with was gone.

I didn't go to work for days. I wasn't in the right frame of mind to teach, and my students deserved more than someone who was just going to let them write their essays in class and learn nothing. I was a shell, and I couldn't pull out of it, right up until Kate texted me to warn me that Sasha was going on a date, and then I snapped out of it.

I was angry. I knew Sasha was trying to move on, but I didn't want her to. All I'd thought about was her since the last time we'd seen each other, and deep down I knew it was the same for her. I knew she was trying to distract herself, but I didn't want her to distract herself. I wanted her to ignore every damn thing that had happened and come back to me. I couldn't believe that she was going to be happy with someone else, as much as she deserved to be. She was meant to be with me, and I was going to actually try to get her back this time. Somehow I would get her back, and this time I wouldn't let her push me away.

# CHAPTER TWELVE
*Sasha*

Slapping Jenna was a bad idea; there was no doubt about it. I felt so terrible, even after everything she'd done. I just felt like slapping her made me a bad person too. Kate tried to tell me it was completely justified, but I just wasn't hearing it. It wasn't justified at all, it was petty and childish.

When we got back to mine, I was feeling the day. My skin felt dry, my eyes felt tired and my legs felt like jelly. Kate suddenly jumped up, telling me she was going to give me something to smile about. I stared at her blankly. "Sasha, why don't we go out tonight?" she said; a question that hovered awkwardly in the air before I finally agreed. I didn't make much of an effort. I took a shower, telling myself I'd be quick, but as the scolding water cascaded down my body, I was aware of how much my body needed the relaxing heat and pummelling texture of the water. I groaned quietly to myself. In just a few short weeks, my life had gone from being perfectly fine and uneventful to being the most stressfully heart-breaking thing I'd ever come across. I found myself wondering what I'd done to piss off the cosmos, and then I started to think that maybe I'm just cursed. I'd never been lucky when it came to guys. So I'd only had two real boyfriends, but there had been plenty of failed conquests before and in between. Guys that didn't like me back, thought I was ugly or not worth their time, and even a couple who just wanted to use me to make the girls they liked jealous. Unlucky in love should've been my tagline, but I kept daydreaming, wishing on stars and hoping that one day I'd meet 'the one' and I really thought I had. Nick had been perfect. Looking into his eyes for the first time had felt like that ridiculously clichéd 'love at first sight' that you always read about and watched in films. It was clichéd but it was there, as strong as electromagnets, pulling me to him like some kind of invisible lasso. Everything with Nick felt right, and it wasn't just that first time that I felt as if I was looking into the eyes of my soul mate, it was every time I looked at him, talked to him or thought about him. I just felt complete and real and right, and thinking about life without him, no matter how short-a-time I'd known him, it felt wrong. I needed something to take my mind off of it all.

We went to Fivers. It wasn't exactly Kate's brightest idea. Being in the club just made me think about that first time we'd seen each other. I remembered the attraction like it was yesterday. I could feel the electricity in my skin when our bodies had touched, the fire in my soul and the way the room had disappeared when we kissed and that nagging sensation of need when we'd pulled away. It was like it was all imprinted on my brain, and all I wanted was to forget it. It was only five o'clock, but for the first time in my life, I wanted a drink. Alcohol tasted like death and depression to me, but it seemed to help people forget, and that was what I wanted. I ordered shots, throwing them back like they were water or at least water that burned my throat and made me feel sick. When I'd had as many shots as I could handle, I moved on to beer. I don't know why I chose beer, but it was just the only thing that popped into my mind when the bartender asked me what it was I wanted next. A little while later I was slumped on the bar feeling much worse for wear and completely out of sorts, and then Nick turned up, and I passed out.

I drifted in and out of consciousness several times, not really taking anything in before blacking out again, and then when I finally did wake up, I was having toast shoved in my face and coffee poured down my throat. I can't say I was complaining, because they actually made me feel a little less like I was on a ferry in the middle of a storm. I was pretty much dead to the world after that.

I woke up surrounded by the scent I'd come to associate with Nick, wrapped in sheets I'd slept in before, in a room I'd admired from the very moment I'd stepped inside, but there was something missing. In the first few moments after I woke up, I couldn't understand why Nick wasn't beside me, and then it all came back to me, along with a pounding headache and a mouth that felt like sandpaper. I wondered if I'd made a fool of myself last night. I have no recollection of getting into this bed, no idea what I'd said, or done, and I had no idea where Nick was. I wanted so desperately for him to be by my side, his arms around me with his bed hair and sleepy eyes, but that would just make things complicated, and if they got any more complicated, neither of us would know what was going on anymore.

I stayed snuggled up in his covers for far longer than I should have, letting myself savour what I knew I couldn't let myself have anymore. I reminisced about our time together, and I tried my hardest to get my head and my heart to come to terms with the fact that we had lost. They couldn't of course, and staying there, keeping my thoughts locked in the past wasn't going to help me at all in the long run, so I finally got up and went to find Nick. He was asleep in the bath, looking completely adorable and irresistible, bundled in blankets with a leg slung casually over the side of the tub and his face smushed against a pillow. I nudged him to wake him and when he opened his eyes, he blinked slowly, causing my heart to melt and shatter at the same time. I did the only thing I could think of. I forced myself to act as if I were angry. I asked him what I was doing there, and when he asked if I didn't remember, I took the line and made it work for my fake anger. I couldn't keep it up though. I saw the hurt in his eyes and I had to be real with him. I could never not be real with him. I told him he couldn't save me anymore, I asked him to take me home, and when he agreed, I felt what was left of my heart fall out of my chest. Finishing with Nick would have me done.

We drove back to mine in silence and I watched him for the entire journey, trying to remember every movement and detail of his being. I made a list of all the things I loved about him in my head. Those eyes, lips, his smile, how he looked at me, his hands, his sense of humour and his eyelashes. The way he knew exactly how I felt and what I was thinking before I even said anything, how strong, caring and sweet he is and how tight he holds me were all on that list, along with a thousand other tiny details. Details such as: how the veins in his wrists would show more vividly when he was tense, and how he never took his eyes off the road for the journey back to mine, but for a split second when he looked over at me and the corners of his mouth twitched sadly. I didn't want this to be the end. I loved him more than anything else in the entire universe, but I had to let go because Jenna was going to keep coming back, and eventually we'd just end up bitter and unhappy all the time. We pulled up just around the corner from mine, and as I got out of the car, I was wondering how I was ever going to say goodbye, but just as I decided not to say goodbye at all, Nick grabbed my wrist. I looked at him, wondering, and finally, he looked at me with the saddest expression. "I love you," he whispered. My shattered and melted heart crumbled even more. It was the first time he'd ever said he loved me, what a goodbye. I linked my fingers with his, and then pulled away from him.

"I love you too," I promised, walking away.

My parents were already awake when I got home, sitting in the kitchen, talking about work and life as if everything that had happened with Nick two days previously was ancient history. "Where have you been?" my dad asked.

"Like you even care," I muttered, turning to go upstairs. He stood up, stopping me in my tracks.

"I know you think we're the worst people in the world Sasha. I know you think you're never going to get over your feelings for this man, but you are. This is nothing but a childish crush, you will grow out of it, and you'll thank us for intervening," he smiled as if that bull was supposed to make me feel better.

"Dad, I don't mean to disrespect you or anything, but you don't know shit about how I feel. Nick isn't my lecturer, of course you still don't believe me, but he's not, and he never was. He was a guy I met and fell in love with. You may not like it, but that's how it is. I'm old enough to know when what I'm feeling is real and what I'm feeling is not 'just a childish crush' and I'd really appreciate it if you'd just let me grieve for my ruined relationship in peace. It's not going away overnight, and if you think it is, then I'm sorry but you've forgotten what it was like to be young and in love, and that's really sad. Now, I'm going to go upstairs now, and take a shower, and then I'm going for a walk, please don't try to stop me." I looked at him for a second, seeing him acknowledge the fact he'd been defeated, and then went on my un-merry way.

The days that followed my drunken faux par were uneventful and filled with depression, and then I got an inbox from an old family friend on Facebook. Clark and I had literally known each other since the day I was born. We'd grown up and spent almost every day together for twelve years, and then he moved and we lost touch, finally getting back in contact about six months ago through Facebook. I'd had a massive crush on him when we were young, but nothing ever came of it. I found it strange how fate had had him message me just days after my breakup, but I was grateful for the distraction.

'Hello trouble! I'm going to be staying near you for a few weeks while I'm on work experience for college, I was wondering if you want to catch up?' he wrote.

'Sounds good to me. Why don't you stop by one evening for dinner and we'll see if we can arrange something?'

'Excellent! Not to be forward, but how's tonight?'

'Tonight is good :)' I smiled to myself, feeling a little weird.

Before Clark arrived, I tried to make myself look relatively presentable. I can't say I made a massive effort because to be honest, I didn't see the point in making an effort for anyone that wasn't Nick. However, I did throw on a little concealer to dim the intensity of the circles under my eyes, a coating of mascara and some lip balm so that I didn't look like I'd skipped out on sleep for the past three months. I then pulled on some random jeans and one of the sweatshirts I'd stolen from Nick. I sighed as I looked at myself in the mirror. The sweatshirt still smelled faintly of Nick, but my own scent was slowly taking over. I was trying not to wear them all too much, but sometimes I just needed to.

Clark looked great. His dark hair was short and a little wavy, nothing like Nick's but it suited him. His green eyes seemed brighter than they had when we were younger and he'd definitely been going to the gym. He hugged me when he walked through the door. It was tight, warm, and safe, but it wasn't a Nick hug. I stifled a sigh and pulled away, offering him a drink before leading him through to the kitchen. "So, how have you been?" he asked, smiling a little awkwardly.

"Not great, long story, how about you?"

"I've been alright. Tell me this long story, I have plenty of time," he pushed. I started to tell him, but the way he was nodding made me suspicious.

"My parents spoke to you didn't they?" I asked. He nodded.

"Yeah. I'm sorry, they called me and it sounded like you were going through a rough time, so I wanted to come and check if you were okay."

"Well, thanks, but I'm fine. My parents just want to butt into my life all of a sudden. They still haven't stopped to ask me what's really going on. It's like they don't give a flying fuck where that letter came from or how fake it was. They just don't want me to be with Nick and *that's final,*" I huffed, mimicking their voices like a child. "This isn't your problem, I'm sorry. I just don't know what to do anymore." I rubbed my temples out of habit and let confusion take over as Clark leaned over and took one of my hands.

"I know I'm not Nick, and you're clearly not ready to move on yet, but why don't you let me buy you a coffee or something while I'm here? We can just talk and maybe take your mind off Nick a little bit," he smiled reassuringly. Part of me wanted to slap him and walk away, but a much more reasonable part knew that he was just being nice, and it wouldn't do me any harm to accept a coffee from an old friend. So I said yes, feeling the weight of the answer on my tongue and my heart. We talked for a while and eventually he left, heading to wherever it was he was going to. After he was gone, I had some time to myself to think about things. Going for a coffee with Clark wouldn't be so bad, and I couldn't just sit around pining after Nick when I couldn't even see him. Except for every time I closed my eyes or let my mind wander just the slightest bit. Who am I kidding? I needed the distraction of something else to worry about before my heart exploded and my head went insane. Nick was the only thing I could think about constantly and he was on my mind 24/7: his smile, his face, his hands and the way his arms felt around me. All of it was plaguing me and I couldn't seem to shake it. I should've been moving on, after all, fate clearly didn't want us to be together, but everything in me was still chasing after the idea that maybe one day we could be and for some reason, I just couldn't let that go. I hoped that taking up Clark on his offer for coffee might just help turn down the frequency of my feelings for Nick.

I lay in bed that night wondering what fate had in store for me. So far it had gifted me with a cheating boyfriend, who then turned into a stalker, the upping and moving of the only life I'd ever known, and the ruining of what felt like love at first sight. Of course, I was being completely selfish. I had made some wonderful friends here, and I had an amazing family, for the most part. Deep down I knew my parents were only trying to protect me, but Nick was all I wanted and with how things had ended, all I could think about was how hard done by I was because I knew I was never going to find a love that matched what I felt for Nick. This was the real deal, everything that mattered, and it was gone. I felt the tears forming, felt my throat tightening and my eyes well up, and it wasn't the hysterical kind of crying or sobbing that I'd experienced over the past few days. It was the slow, mournful kind of crying that told me Nick and I were over, and it hurt more than any other kind of pain ever could. I curled into a ball in the pitch black dark, and I fell asleep to the sounds of the chinking chains around my heart.

# CHAPTER THIRTEEN

*Nick*

After making the decision that I needed to get Sasha back, I kind of had to come up with a plan, and it took me far too long to come up with a good one, but by the time I had everything set in place, I was confident it would work. I was back at work, trying desperately to get my classes back on track after whoever had replaced me had completely messed up my lesson plans, and I was throwing myself all in. If I wasn't teaching, I was marking. If I wasn't marking, I was planning lessons weeks in advance, and when I wasn't doing those things, I was trying not to be nervous about the fact that I was just casually going to try to butt in on my shouldn't-be-ex girlfriend's date. I had the day and the coffee shop noted. Now all I needed was the time, which Kate was currently working on finding out. I guess it helped to have Sasha's best friend on my side, but I felt kind of skeevy messing with the fates just to realign them.

On the morning of the first date, I was feeling weird. It felt kind of stalkery to be finding out the exact times and places of Sasha's dates just to prove to her that we were meant to be together, but this plan was as much Kate's idea as it was mine. So if I was going down, I wouldn't be going down alone. I wore the sweatshirt Sasha had borrowed the night we'd jumped in the ocean that she'd only recently exchanged for a darker grey one, and the black jeans that she always said she loves on me. I was ready to be sneaky, and although some part of me was trying to tell me it was a bad idea, the rest of me was totally okay with it.

I arrived at Starbucks about ten minutes early. I had my laptop, a small pile of marking, and my heavily battered and dog-eared copy of Romeo and Juliet to make it look as if I was just casually marking in Starbucks, which I kind of was. I ordered a vanilla latte and dumped a ton of cinnamon on top before stirring it in, and then I settled in for the ride. Sasha and her 'date' arrived well after the time Kate said they would but I was glad. I was so wrapped up in my work that at first, I didn't even realise they'd entered the shop, this bode well for me, considering it genuinely looked as if I was just doing my work there, and not trying to psych Sasha out. Her date ordered their coffee while she stood awkwardly beside him, not showing her usually confident sparkiness, and then she saw me probably staring like an idiot. A small smile formed on her face, her eyes lit up when they met mine as she walked towards me, a little dazed, and then stopped herself about a metre away. "Nick, what are you doing here?" she asked, trying to sound formal, even though her voice hinted at curiosity.

"My Wi-Fi dropped out last night and I needed some internet to get my work done. If I'd known you would be here, I'd have chosen somewhere else," I muttered, watching her face sink a little. I felt bad for that.

"Oh, why is your Wi-Fi down?"

"I don't know, I called the provider, but they told me it would be back within forty eight hours, so we'll see." I frowned, remembering that we wouldn't see at all. This was so awkward, and I know she felt it. Her date came over just then, looking like a stereotypical American teen movie actor, not that I was jealous or anything. She introduced us, her face reddening a little in the process of the name exchange.

"Uh, Nick, this is Clark, he's an old friend, and Clark, this is Nick..." she trailed off. I was glad she was referring to this Clark person as 'an old friend' instead of her new boyfriend or something, but I felt a stabbing in my general heart area when she didn't explain who I was, but that was fine. I didn't plan on Clark not knowing who I was for very long. I extended my hand as I said, "Nice to meet you," and then apologised for having to get back to my work quite promptly. Sasha cocked her head to the side as her brows furrowed, then her face regained its composure and she walked to the furthest empty table she could find, waiting for Clark to follow. I smiled to myself a little, knowing my plan was already working. Now it was time for step two. That would take a little more time to set into motion. I stuck around for another half an hour, finding it surprisingly productive, getting my work done somewhere different for once, and then I left, as quietly as possible, hoping Sasha would somehow notice my presence had disappeared.

Phase two of getting Sasha back was going to emotionally pain me. I knew it as soon as Kate suggested it. Kate's idea was to have me turn up at the same restaurant with a date of my own. I felt like this plan was cruel, it was false, and it would be unfair on whoever I was taking on the 'date' as well as on Sasha and myself. However, Kate was adamant that this was the only way I could make Sasha see that she didn't actually want to be with anyone else.

The days leading up to 'the date' were nerve-racking and stressful. Cat and Kate were basically holding open auditions for my date, trying to find the best match that would make Sasha jealous. I didn't really want to take part, but they made me sit in on the interviews. Every single person that turned up was a model friend of Cat's, meaning that most of them acted like vapid narcissists with no personalities because they'd been taught to act that way by their mothers, feeding off their daughters' fame. A few of them actually showed signs of intelligence, intellectuality and personality, and those were the ones that made the shortlist. Everything about this process seemed so wrong, but Cat told me her friends were looking at this as a job, something to help out with their acting for future ad auditions, and that made me feel a little less like a pig.

Eventually, we narrowed the search down to one girl, Harriet. She was only about two inches shorter than me without heels, had doll-like lips, brown, cat-like eyes or maybe that was just the makeup talking. Her hair was shiny, straight and light brown. She had a sense of humour, which was nice and she knew a lot about books. We spent a while getting to know each other, to make our date more convincing, and I actually found out that she was mostly helping me out so that she could make her ex-boyfriend want her back, which was all the more helpful to me.

We had a few crash courses on things we should know about each other before the date, like favourite colours, jobs, tv shows, films, music and food. This was done just so that we could make the date seem more authentic, and then we booked our table at the restaurant.

On the night of the date, I was nervous. My shirt was crisp, my trousers were ironed (thanks to Cat) and my tie was far too tight, so I took it off. I picked Harriet up from her hotel and then we made our way to the restaurant. Our reservation was booked for half an hour after Sasha's, which would apparently mean she'd see us walk in. This time I wasn't supposed to make eye contact, I wasn't supposed to acknowledge Sasha until she acknowledged me, but when I saw her through the window of the restaurant, my entire mind just melted. She was wearing a sparkly black dress that was hugging her figure in the most seductive way, with her white converse that I don't think I've ever seen her without. The only thing that was different was her hair. She'd straightened it instead of letting it curl like she usually did. It just threw me off. I suppressed a sigh and opened the door, letting Harriet go through in front of me. The waitress seated us about four tables down from Sasha and Clark. We were in the corner on our own, a candle between us and drinks on the way. Sasha hadn't spotted me yet and I was starting to think that this was probably just a massive waste of time and effort. Then out of the corner of my eye, I saw her head turn, and then I saw her stand up and started walking towards us. I tried to regulate my breathing and calm my nerves before she got to the table, but she knew me so well that I was sure she would know there was something fishy going on. "Nick, what're you doing here?" she asked, her eyes boring into mine as if she knew exactly what I was up to.

I cleared my throat, "Uh, I'm on a date," I replied, feeling guilty as the corners of her mouth turned down. She smoothed out her dress and straightened her back a little.

"I see. Well, have fun," she smiled, walking back to her table and running a hand through her hair when she sat down, something she always did when she was stressed. I felt terrible. This was the worst idea and I should never have asked for Kate's help in getting Sasha back. Girls are so scheming, they're trained to plan and deceive from a young age by TV shows, books and magazines, but us guys just aren't cut out for this. Harriet asked if I was okay and I nodded, not wanting to let a stranger into more of my life than I already have.

"I'm great, but we should probably just give up," I admitted; hoping fiercely that she would agree.

"I'm here to help you get your girlfriend back. We won't stop until you get that," she told me, winking and giggling loudly all of a sudden, twirling her hair and looking at me as if I were the ruler of the earth.

"What are you doing?" I whispered, rubbing my temple nervously, just wanting to get the bill and go home.

"Just laugh, she's watching us and she looks jealous," Harriet grinned.

"I don't want her to be jealous. This was a stupid idea," I said, feeling completely helpless when Harriet took my hand across the table. I quickly pulled my hand away, making my mind up to just get the bill and leave when Sasha stopped me in my tracks.

"Why are you really here?" she asked, looking furious.

"What do you mean?"

"Look, you're clearly not enjoying your 'date', so why are you here?"

"Just because we had a bit of a disagreement doesn't mean I'm not having a good time..." I paused, suddenly spurred on by her anger. "But wait, you're allowed to date freely, but I'm not?"

"I never said that." She shook her head. "I just didn't peg you for the type of guy that goes with just about anything he can find."

"Can you hear yourself right now Sash? Can you hear what you're saying?" I knew she was acting out because she still cared, and a part of me felt good about that, but another part of me got caught up in the drama, and I wanted her to know how much her dating someone else was hurting me. "Why do you have a right to insult my date, while you're off on your own little adventure? How is that okay? You ended things, not me. It wasn't what I wanted at all, so why are you causing trouble for me while I'm trying to move on?" I asked, actually standing up to face her properly. We were probably causing the most ridiculous scene. She pinched the bridge of her nose.

"Nick, you being here isn't exactly helping *me* move on, is it? This was exactly my point, exactly my reasoning when we broke up. You can take this girl out, you can flaunt her and hold her hand, but we couldn't do that because of Jenna. We maybe would've never had the chance to do that, and that wasn't right, but now you being here with this girl, do you think that doesn't hurt me? I need to move on Nick. This isn't easy for us, but I need to because I know that you and I will never work with that dragon breathing down our necks and constantly threatening to set another of our houses on fire. You were in the coffee shop, and I let that go, but I can't put this down to coincidence. This has Kate's name written all over it. I should know, I would've done the same thing, but we're over now Nick, and you need to just let me move on." She locked eyes with me for a second before walking back to her table and sitting down as if nothing had happened. I glared at Harriet, feeling all the worse for wear and asked the waitress for the bill. I paid it, tipped her and then left the restaurant, only waiting for Harriet when I was actually in the car. She eventually joined me, looking guilty.

"I'm sorry for pushing it. I should've toned it down when you started freaking out." I started the car without speaking, not wanting her to hear the anger in my voice.

Eventually I spoke, "It was never a good plan to begin with. It's fine." Harriet nodded, probably realising I just needed some peace and quiet. The only time she spoke was just before we reached her hotel.

“I’m sorry the plan didn’t work. If it’s any consolation, she still clearly cares for you. If it’s meant to be, I’m sure she’ll come to her senses. Don’t give up on her just yet. She’s just trying to find a way to adjust to her feelings, don’t let go of her, just give her some space before you go barrelling back in. It might just help.” She then smiled reassuringly and I actually did feel reassured. Who knew Harriet would show signs of being a true friend.

“I’m worried that if I leave her too long, she’ll move on. She’s already getting on with this Clark bloke. I just don’t want her to end up with him, or anyone else but me. It’s selfish but it doesn’t feel over.” My voice faltered.

“If she ends up with someone else, it wasn’t meant to be, but if it’s worth anything, I don’t think she will.” Harriet patted my shoulder and got out of the car. “I’ll see you around Nick, I really hope things work out.” I nodded and waited until she was in the hotel lobby to drive away.

I threw my keys on the kitchen table when I got in and grabbed a beer from the fridge. I didn’t bother turning the main lights on. I just switched on the lamp for the extractor fan and sat on my own in the semi darkness. I knew Kate's plan hadn't been fool proof. There were flaws all over the place and I never should have gone through with it, but I only had myself to blame for everything that had happened tonight, and now I had to deal with it. I felt a huge weight on my heart, dragging me deeper into this vortex of darkness that had been looming upon me since Sasha said her first goodbye. I was trying so damn hard not to let it consume me but I was already knee deep and I hadn't realised. I dropped my head to the table and groaned. What was I supposed to do now? Where was I supposed to go from here? It seemed so weird to think that not long ago, I didn't even know Sasha existed, but now she was my entire life. She was everything I wanted and needed and nothing else mattered to me but I was in the process of losing her, and I'd only made sure of that by trying to keep her. I couldn't help but hate Jenna with a passion.

I don't remember going to bed that night. I just remember waking up to an empty bed that still smelled faintly of Sasha's shampoo. She was slowly disappearing from my life and it didn't feel as if there was any way for me to get her back. I was losing her and I was losing myself too.

# CHAPTER FOURTEEN
*Sasha*

Mine and Clark's coffee date was pleasant and weird all at the same time, and the fact that Nick was in Starbucks when we arrived kind of threw me off. When he told me he was there because his Wi-Fi was down, all I wanted to do was find out how and why and ask him what marking he was doing and if he needed me to help out. But then I remembered that we were broken up, that I was out for coffee with someone else, and then I was aware that I felt incredibly depressed about the fact. In a way, I just wanted to sit next to Nick with a coffee and watch him work but I was here with Clark, and I had to get over Nick.

After Clark and Nick had awkwardly met each other, I found Clark and myself a table and then I tried to forget about the absolutely wonderful, beautiful, attractive and completely perfect man sitting at his laptop far away from me but still in my line of vision I instead focused on the cute friend who had always been there for me. It wasn't easy. The way Nick worked, the way he focused and smiled when he saw a line he liked in an essay made me feel flustered and foggy. I kept mixing up my words and losing my train of thought while I talked to Clark and eventually, he had to ask why. I told him it was just me being silly, but being the great friend he is, he didn't buy it. "If he's distracting you so much, turn away, you don't have to look at him," Clark said, smiling slightly.

"Good plan," I said as I shifted my chair. It didn't help much. Not being able to see Nick just made me feel more uncomfortable, but I did at least manage to pull myself together enough to have an actual conversation. We talked about everything we could possibly think of, jobs, college, favourite colours, films, books, and food, so basically everything that had changed since we'd last seen each other properly. It wasn't really a date: more like a catch up with an old friend. Everything was going fine until I heard the door open and close, feeling somewhere deep inside me as if Nick had left, I turned to check and I was right. Sighing, I shifted my chair back to its original position and pretty much tuned out on Clark for a good ten minutes before he asked if I was even listening. I shook my head guiltily and asked him if it would be okay for us to leave, I wasn't really feeling Starbucks any more.

We got back to mine far too early for my parents not to ask questions but considering the fact I still wasn't speaking to them, they were never answered. I didn't want to invite Clark up to my room. Nick had never even seen my room, and I didn't want Clark to get the wrong idea, so we went to my dad's office. The place was filled with books and had always been one of my favourite places, whether it was the office he'd had back in our old house or this one; it was the books that made it feel homely to me. I asked Clark if he wanted a drink, heading to the mini fridge in the corner to grab myself a diet coke, and him a regular. He asked if I had anything stronger, so I pulled a large dictionary off of one of the shelves, opening it up to reveal a small, half full bottle of vodka that my dad had given me in secret when I'd turned sixteen. He knew I didn't drink, but he told me it would never hurt to have it, just in case I needed to win anyone over. It had always been a little joke between us, and the only person that had ever actually used my little gift had been Kate. I grabbed a tumbler from on top of the mini fridge and handed him the coke and the vodka. "Don't you want any?" he asked. I shook my head, telling him I didn't drink and laughed a little when a look of shock shadowed his face.

"It's no big deal," I smiled. "I just don't really like alcohol," I shrugged. It really wasn't a big deal and I still have no clue why everyone wanted to make it into one. Clark let it lie after a little teasing and then he hit me where it hurt, accidentally.

"So, that Nick guy is a little smart," he stated, pulling a face and making me instantly jump to Nick's defence.

"He probably came straight from work. There's no need to be rude about it," I uttered.

"You clearly still have feelings for him, Sasha, it was a joke," he smirked, making me realise I should've known he was joking.

"Well, I'm not like you, Clark, I can't get over someone in a day, but I'm trying. It's not like we can get back together anyway. It's done."

"So you want to get over him by dating me, right?"

"Don't make me out to be a bad guy here. I never asked you to invite me to coffee, and I certainly don't expect you to take me out again, but I do need to get myself out there. People are always going to try to get in between us, so I need to move on, sooner rather than later," I huffed, crossing my arms over my chest defensively.

"You really don't have to explain yourself to me, and I don't mind being your rebound. In fact, I'd be honoured to take you out again if you'd like?" He asked politely. My heart told me no. I felt physically sick at the thought of moving on but it had to be done. So I ignored my heart and I nodded, telling him he should call me to arrange a day and a time.

Eventually Clark left and I was nothing but relieved. I didn't want to make small talk or hear him insult Nick anymore. I just wanted to be alone to wallow in my own sadness, to sleep and dream about blissful times with Nick, which I know is totally bad for me and not helping me get over him at all It's just that he looked so amazing tonight, and I couldn't help but lay in my bed daydreaming about what could've happened if I wasn't on a coffee date and Nick and I hadn't broken up. But we had, and every single time I started to daydream, I had to remind myself of that because I couldn't carry on living in the past or living in daydreams. It wasn't going to help me and it wasn't going to make the past come back, so I had to stop, and that's what I worked on through the night while I couldn't sleep. I worked on cleansing my mind of daydreams of Nick and when they slipped through, I worked on scenarios where I was strong enough to walk away and I guess, in the hypothetical world, it worked.

The next few days were hell. I was over-tired and almost delirious through everything I did. Work dragged on and usually I loved it but I couldn't even concentrate on conversations with people. I don't know why I couldn't sleep or what was keeping me up, but I decided to take a day off from everything and just catch up on my sleep. I slipped into bed, and knowing that I had absolutely nothing to do that day, actually seemed to help, because the next thing I knew, it was dark outside and I was starving.

I stumbled downstairs in the dark and flipped on the kitchen light. I then raided the fridge and made myself a quick sandwich, sitting down at the island to wolf it down and have a read of the local newspaper. Nothing interesting was going on, except that a sudden influx of apparently well-known models had been checking into the higher rated hotels in town. I wondered if there was some model event that no one knew about. I thought about phoning Cat, but I had no idea what Nick had told her about our breakup, so I didn't want to make things awkward. "Blah," I muttered into the empty room, before sticking the paper in the cupboard under the sink for any future artistic endeavours. No one really paid any attention to that cupboard usually. It was filled with a neat stack of newspapers, a litre sized tub of PVA glue, several boxes of various sized ice lolly sticks and a shit ton of different types of paint and paint brushes. It was my little cupboard of artistic treasure, and I couldn't believe I'd left it untouched for so long. I'd always drawn or painted when I didn't know what I was doing or where I was going, but I'd completely neglected my creativity while I'd been floating around just waiting for a sign to point me in the right direction. I smiled to myself, heading back to my arts and crafts cupboard and pulling out a sketch pad, a tin of pencils and a rubber. I went into the living room and over to the sofa, curling a leg underneath myself while the other dangled to the floor. I reached behind me to flick on one of the many lamps we had in there, and then I began to sketch out my feelings. I wasn't really thinking about what I was drawing, I just was, and when I was done, I saw an image of a boy and a girl under lights in a club, kissing like their lives depended on it. I put it down to my subconscious mind wanting something to draw, and then I sat staring at the drawing for a while. I actually liked it, despite it having an uncanny resemblance to me and Nick, it wasn't a horrible drawing, and the process of getting it done did help to chill me out.

I woke up the next morning feeling pretty positive, until I got a text from Clark asking when I wanted to schedule our date for. I told him I was free Friday night, and he told me he'd pick me up at seven. I then called Kate for advice.

"Hey!" she said chirpily, picking up on the second ring.

"Hi."

"You don't sound happy, why?"

"Well, Clark asked me on another date, and, well, I don't know if it's just leading him on when I'm not over Nick?" I said around a mouthful of coco pops.

"He said he didn't mind being the rebound, right? So it's fine, just go with the flow, and see how things turn out. You're set on moving on, so actually put yourself out there and get it done. Clark seems like a tough dude, he can take it. When are you going out anyway?" I told her she was right, and then I gave her the time and day of the date, just so she could phone me to talk about it afterwards, and then we just spoke about random stuff. She told me she was gutted that my suspension wasn't up for another week, because class was boring without drama of course; and she told me that Jenna had been getting all kinds of questions thrown at her by students since I'd been away. The news didn't exactly make me happy. It just made me think about how much Jenna had taken away from me. She was supposed to be someone to be trusted, and she turned out to be the kind of person to use her power to control others. I sighed, getting ready for work and leaving without a word to my parents. I didn't know exactly how long I was going to freeze them out, but I was still upset over how they'd point blank refused to hear my explanation and I didn't see any point in letting them off the hook when they'd make no move to de-hook themselves anyway.

The day of the date came around and I was almost shaking with nerves. I decided I'd give myself a makeover to pass the time and calm the nerves, but all I was really doing was making myself up into someone else. I could play a role better than I could play myself at times like these. I jumped in the shower and deep conditioned my hair after I washed it, and then I dried and straightened it to within an inch of its life. My hair hadn't been straightened since before I'd met Nick. I just didn't feel the need to be anything but natural when I was around him, and now here I was, getting ready for a date with someone who wasn't him, and making myself into someone I'm not. I scoured my wardrobe for something elegant but still stylish, and settled on a tight, black, strapless dress that was made up of sparkles and tiny black beads. It had a silk slip attached underneath with black netting for the skirt. I wore nude tights and then shoved on my white converse without even thinking about it. From there, I smoked out my eyes with greys, blacks and a hint of purple, and ran a nude lip gloss over my lips. The girl staring back at me in the mirror certainly wasn't my usual self, but she looked fine nonetheless.

Everything was going fine. From the moment Clark picked me up, everything was pleasant, right up until I noticed Nick sitting at a table in the corner of the restaurant with some random girl. I tried to ignore them, but eventually I had to confront him. I went over to ask why he was here, and when he told me he was on a date, I felt like I'd been punched in the gut with a barge poll. I swallowed the lump in my throat and told him to have fun, and then went to join Clark again. I was trying my best to just focus on my own date, but when I heard ridiculously loud giggling coming from Nick's corner of the restaurant, I couldn't do it anymore. I looked around at the exact moment Nick snatched his hand away from the girl he was with, and that's when I smelled something fishy. I started towards Nick but almost collided with him when he stood up. I confronted him, asking him what he was really doing here. At first he feigned ignorance, but I repeated my question, knowing better than to back down. Nick really confronted me then, asking why I was causing trouble for him when he was trying to move on, and I really didn't have an answer. It dawned on me then, that both times Nick had showed up, Kate had known exactly when and where I'd be. Then I remembered the countless times we'd watched Gossip Girl and dreamed of scheming like those fictional upper east siders. I knew then that this wasn't so much Nick's idea, as Kate's, and I didn't blame her, because I would truly have done the same to try and make her happy. I backed down after telling Nick that he needed to let me move on, and then I went back to Clark. We ate in silence and left right after making it back to mine with less than a few words.

When we stepped through my front door, the house was quiet and the lights were off. I flicked a few on and then I lead us both into the kitchen, slamming my tiny bag down on the table and kicking the bottom of the fridge. "So, that was eventful," Clark commented, making me feel awful.

"Look Clark, I'm sorry. I can't do this. I can't lead you on. I can't let you be my rebound because you deserve better than that, and if I'm honest, I don't think you really like me as much as you think you do. Clark, we've been friends for as long as I've been alive, and I don't want to jeopardise that for a few rebound dates, okay?" Clark smiled at me after my little speech and then reached across the counter to grab my hand.

"I'm glad you've finally realised you can't do this. I knew it from the start babes. You just needed to see it for yourself. I like you, I really do, but you're right, it's not worth risking our friendship over, especially when you're madly in love with someone else, even if you won't accept that." He squeezed my hand and then turned to leave. "I'll call you for a decent catch up soon, okay?" I nodded, smiling at his back as he let himself out, and then I grabbed my phone and called Kate to give her hell.

Kate didn't even argue when I accused her of being a scheming bitch, she just agreed with me and then asked if I'd learned my lesson. I thought about it for a moment and thanked her for getting involved. "I'm glad to hear my pesky meddling actually helped you realise that going out with Clark was a bad idea, but we haven't really talked about you and Nick since everything happened. I think we need to," Kate said, seriously.

"I just don't know where to start to be honest. I know what I want to say, but I can't get the words out," I admitted.

"Then how about we go for a girly weekend?" she suggested, making me nod. Until I realised she couldn't see me.

"Sounds good," I said, truthfully and then we made some arrangements for the week after before hanging up.

I felt less on edge that night. Knowing I was going to have a weekend away soon and some time to just detox made my mind just chill a little, and I also didn't have the added worry of not hurting the rebound.

# CHAPTER FIFTEEN
*Nick*

Trying to give up on Sasha was one of the hardest things I'd ever had to do, and I'd had to do a lot of hard things. Even just her name still sent shivers down my spine and put an enormous smile on my face, but she was right. We both needed to move on now. She didn't want to be with me because she didn't think Jenna would ever stop her meddling, and I couldn't get back together with someone who was determined not to be with me. It hurt a lot. Knowing Sasha was walking around out there, having these feelings for me but trying to forget me. The thought of her not liking me like that anymore made me feel completely numb, but I could understand her reasoning, I really could.

I spent a lot of time diving into my work. I re-wrote all of my lesson plans, coming up with better, more exciting ways to teach my students about the star crossed lovers and their ultimate doom; trying not to relate their gruesome end to the slightly messy breakup Sasha and I had left behind. CJ tried to make me feel better. He brought beers to the flat and listened to music and watched films, but I never really felt myself. Not at all, and when they thought I wasn't around or wasn't listening, CJ and Cat would talk about me, as if I were a child that wouldn't behave right. I locked myself away a lot. I started on my second, secret novel, a sequel to the first, and listened to new music that I'd probably never have discovered if it weren't for my new found YouTube addiction. I was acting like a heartbroken teenager, but then I got to thinking. Everyone does one of two things when they're heartbroken. They either shut themselves away and become almost recluse until they feel like they can face the world again, or they go out every night and drink until they can't feel the pain anymore, and doing that wasn't a teenage thing, it was just a heartbreak thing.

Moving on was harder. I didn't want to go on dates, and I didn't want to go out and meet people. CJ thought it was wrong of me to stay away from girls, seeing as I'd met Sasha because I'd been looking for someone new, but I just wasn't ready. Nothing felt right without her, and it had only actually been a week since we'd argued in the restaurant. I sighed a lot, I marked papers, I watched films and I moped, right up until Kate came to see me.

It was Thursday night and it was raining hard outside. I was all set for the night. Music, laptop, junk food and a supersize bottle of Pepsi waited for me in my room while Cat had some model friends over. I was starting to wonder why she hadn't started to crave her glamorous life yet, but I actually enjoyed having the one family member I could fully depend on around. I was just opening the half written sequel to my novel when I heard a knock on the front door. It was evident that Cat wasn't going to get it, so I pulled myself up from my bed, threw on a grey t-shirt and went to answer the door. When I saw Kate, I groaned, I'll admit. She'd already caused me to lose the tiny shred of Sasha I had left in my life, and now she was back to put me through further hell. Or at least, that's what I thought.

I let Kate head to the kitchen while I went to grab a sweatshirt to shield me from the chill of the tiled room. "What do you want?" I asked, a little rudely. "Nice mood you've got there. Okay, what if I said, I had a solution to your situation?" she grinned, looking hopeful and causing me to shake my head vigorously.

"Nope, no, definitely not. Your ideas have not helped me at all in the past couple of weeks, and all they've done is manage to push me as far away from Sasha as I can possibly get without leaving town. So *please* do not involve me in any more of your crazy plans."

"Okay, my past ideas have been poorly planned and not very well thought out, but this one will work, I promise you. Sasha is miserable without you, and it's not right that you two spend any more time apart. You love each other, through all the problems you could possibly face, and through all the problems you have faced. You love each other, and no one, not even yourselves can stand in the way of that for long. So please, just think about it, and let me know if you're prepared to hear me out." Kate smiled, standing up to leave and letting herself out before I could even respond.

The fact that Kate had decided to walk away and let me decide for myself instead of pressuring me into going along with her plan actually really bugged me. It struck me as weird that she was thinking so much about everyone else that she wasn't even going to argue with me when I accused her of being the reason I couldn't even see Sasha anymore. I decided to talk to CJ and Cat at some point to ask what they thought of the situation, but until then, I was determined to write a bit more and not stew over the current temptation of yet another possibility of getting Sasha back.

I fell asleep at around three in the morning and woke up at around six for work. I was knackered, but my new found appreciation for how work could take my mind off things was spurring me on well enough. I showered quickly and pulled on some black trousers, a white pin striped shirt and a black tie. I wore my usual work shoes and headed to the kitchen to grab some breakfast. Cat was already up, so I took the opportunity to ask her what she thought about Kate's offer. "Kate's a great girl, and while she tends to mess up a bit when she tries to help people, the point is, she tries to help. She has a good heart, and I don't think she'd keep trying if she didn't think Sasha needed you in her life. I know you won't listen to me until you get CJ to back up this point, but think about it before you give up a chance to make it work, okay? I don't like to see you moping around and being all 'blah'. It really doesn't suit you," she smiled, taking her coffee and a bowl of cereal into the living room and leaving me to think about what she'd said. She was right though, I wouldn't really take it on board unless CJ agreed with her.

When I got to work, the place was too quiet to be normal. I went to let myself in through the barriers, but my pass card wouldn't work. I went to the front desk and saw a sea of students and lecturers alike trying to get some information. I spotted CJ pretty quickly, him being taller than your average giant and all. "What's going on?" I asked as I approached him, swerving to avoid some particularly over-excited teenagers. He shrugged, about to speak, but stopped to scold some of his students for mucking about.

"I have no idea mate, but if they don't tell us soon, I'm going to get my car, drive it through the front window and give them an actual reason to be keeping people waiting," I laughed. CJ had never been a patient person. I could actually believe he'd do something drastic just to get an answer in times like this. I waded my way to the front, spying Adella, a girl who had gone to university with us and waved her over to ask what was going on. She shook her head angrily and whipped her phone out of her blouse pocket.

"Someone came into the college last night and vandalised at least two, if not more classrooms on every floor. Some are useable, but most of them are trashed." She paused to show me pictures of the damage. "I'm really sorry, but your room took a pretty good hit, as well as CJ's and mine. Gi's is fine on our floor, but hers is about the only one. It looks completely random, so whoever it was didn't really have a plan, although I'm pretty sure that once we take inventory, we'll discover we've been robbed. As for now, you and CJ are pretty much free to go. We're cancelling lessons today, but we need some crowd control before we tell the students." I nodded, feeling a little gutted that someone had trashed my classroom, but knowing anything that was damaged would most likely be replaced. I just hoped my desk was okay, which was probably a really selfish thought. I told Adella that CJ and I would get some crowd control going with a few of the other lost looking lecturers, and left her to go back to manning reception. We stood on chairs in the reception area while CJ and I whistled loudly to catch people's attention. CJ shouted for the crowds to quieten down and then left me to explain the situation without giving away the full gist of what was going on. Between us and the other lecturers who were still milling about, we managed to get the students out without causing much more of a scene, and then CJ and I headed into town to see if there was anything worth doing. By the time we hit Costa he was asking me what was on my mind, because apparently, recently, I'm as open as the books I read.

"Well," I began, "Kate says she has another new plan and she thinks this one will definitely get me and Sasha on speaking terms. Cat thinks I should at least hear her out, but I'm not sure." I told the barista what I wanted and then waited at the end for CJ to catch up. We both grabbed our drinks and started adding sugar while CJ thought over what I'd told him.

"Do you really think Kate can be trusted to glue the shards of your relationship back together mate? She might only be trying to help, but so far it hasn't exactly gone well, has it? It's just driving you further away from her."

"I know it hasn't worked out so far, but I'm wondering if it might this time. She just seemed so sure that she has a fool proof plan this time. Maybe it'd work?"

There was a question in my voice like I was asking CJ's permission to have hope. I realised then that my mind was completely scrambled, and it had been from the minute Sasha and I had broken up. I'd not been myself since the second we parted ways, and I needed to get my head together. CJ gave me that sympathetic look that I'd gotten used to recently. "If you're not prepared to give up, and you're not ready to let her go, then you have nothing to lose but your own heart. This is entirely up to you. You can't be certain that it's going to work, and by the looks of you right now man, I'm not sure how much more you can take, but you need to do what you need to do, or you'll end up regretting it no matter what happens. You'll kick yourself for never knowing if it could've worked out, and that's a huge mistake to be making, especially with a girl like Sash." CJ dumped his empty coffee cup into a nearby bin and asked me to wait for him while he got some money out. I had that short time to make up my mind, and it went back and forth a few times before I really could make the decision, but eventually I made it.

By the time I got home, it had been dark for about an hour. The lights in the flat were all off and Cat had left a short note telling me she'd probably be back tomorrow. I text Kate telling her I was prepared to hear her out and then sat around stewing while I waited for her to arrive. I don't know why the idea of trying once more made me so nervous, but I had the idea that maybe it was just because I was so desperate for it to work that I couldn't quite cope with it all.

Kate finally arrived just in time for me to finish the pizza I'd shoved in the oven, and I felt a little bad that I hadn't saved any to offer her. She sat at the kitchen table while I made her a drink, and when I sat down opposite her, I didn't really know what to say, but luckily Kate was a woman of many words.

"You look like you're about to lay an egg," she stated.

"Yeah, well, the thought that if this latest plan of yours fails, then that's it, just sets me on edge," I admitted.

"That's sweet, but what you're about to hear isn't, and it's not going to be easy to listen to, so brace yourself," she paused, checking my eyes for confirmation that I was ready to hear her out. I just nodded. "Sasha is not in a good place. She was trying to rebound with Clark but my plans to get you in the way basically broke her and I feel so terrible about that. Her and Clark have decided not to carry things on, which you're probably happy to hear, but she's not in the best place. She's angry, upset, probably depressed, but I'm not an expert. She's still not speaking to her parents, she's running away from everything, hiding in her room and listening to a playlist of songs that makes her bawl as if that's going to make her better. I've never seen Sasha so weak. She's always, always been the strong one, the one to hold everyone together and when she met you, it was like that intensified. She was even more confident, bolder, she smiled twice as much and her advice got even better than it was before, but now it's like she's a shadow of herself. Like you're part of her and you've been gone so long she's forgotten who she is. She's not herself." She stopped there and took in my sad eyes and what I imagined would be a frown on my lips. "So,

I invited her to a girls' weekend. It's at a spa, there's a B&B, and it's all very sophisticated. What I propose, is that you go instead of me. Turn up, I won't say anything, it'll just be you two. What happens is up to the both of you, but it's worth a try. I know I keep saying it, but it's the truth, and it's up to you whether you take me up on it or not. I won't even know until she either phones me to ask where I am or phones me to scream at me for sending you. I'll text you the location, all you have to do is decide if you're going to be there. She'll arrive tomorrow." Kate stood up, feeling no need to elaborate, apparently, and once again, let herself out. Once she'd left, I sat at the kitchen table on my own for a while, before deciding to have a shower and make some serious life decisions.

I finally decided on what I needed to do. It was a long, long process. I was indecisive. On one hand, I could have everything I wanted if I jumped in the car and went on my way. I could have Sasha in my arms, tell her how I feel and tell her that nothing matters when she's not around. I could finally be happy, I could stop running away from my life and my feelings because Sasha knew me, and what she didn't know, I could tell her. On the other hand, I could turn up and Sasha could turn me away again. She could tell me, once again that she needed me to let her move on. She could tell me she couldn't cope with being us, while Jenna was still trying to sabotage things. She could end up making me feel even worse than I already did by ending things for real. Or, she could be so angry that she'll never want to speak to me again.

The options went around in my head, over and over again until I felt like I couldn't think about them any longer, so when I was finally exhausted, I slept, and dreamed about those options further in my subconscious. When I woke up on Saturday morning, the decision was made.

# CHAPTER SIXTEEN
*Sasha*

I was really looking forward to the girls' weekend. I had it in my head that it was just what I needed to cheer me up and help me move on. I packed my bags, and on Friday night, I finally turned off the sad songs playlist, stopped moping and went to talk to my parents. They were incredibly surprised to see me, and I felt sheepish when I went to say what I needed to say. I stood by the sofa, in a place where they could both see me, and then I spoke. I tried to avoid eye contact for the most part, and probably fidgeted way too much to be normal.

"Guys, I know I've acted like a brat these past few weeks, and I know it couldn't have been easy having me ignore you. It hasn't been easy for me either, but the truth is, I needed you to believe me when that letter came through, and you didn't. I can promise you that what I'm about to say is one hundred percent the truth, and you need to hear me out before you pass even more judgement over me and my life," I paused, catching my breath. "That letter, it was fake. It was written by my English Lit lecturer, who just so happens to be, wait for it, Nick's ex-girlfriend, and, regrettably, the woman I punched. Before you ask, yes, the same woman who purposely tampered with my essay. She was messing with me and Nick for a while before she finally sent that letter to you. Nick never was and never will be my lecturer. We met at Fivers, and yes, we probably shouldn't have met up again, but we did, and we were perfect. It's over now, and that's partially because of you, and that's why I ignored you. But I'm going away this weekend with Kate, and I didn't want to spend another weekend not talking, so this is me, waving the white flag, even though I shouldn't have to." I blinked back tears, remembering everything we'd been through as a family and everything they'd done for me. My dad smiled, telling me everything would be okay in the end, and that I'd find someone new eventually, which actually stung a little, because quite frankly, I didn't want to find someone else, or move on. I wanted to stay stuck in this little bubble where it might be possible to one day get back together with Nick, even if I'd stopped it from ever really happening. My mum just stood up and hugged me, telling me she was glad we were on good terms again. I smiled, sat with them for a while, and then told them I had to head to bed before my drive tomorrow.

Upon waking up the next day, I felt kind of weird. The night before had been a relief, getting back on good terms with my parents, but I knew getting fully back into Kate's good books after acting like a total moron for the past couple of weeks was going to be much, much harder. I jumped in the shower, letting the scolding hot water caress my skin like tiny tongues of fire, and then realised I'd spent far too much time in there and was going to be late if I didn't leave soon. I threw my towel dried hair up into a messy bun, grabbed my overnight bags and headed straight to the car.

The drive was long and pretty boring considering I had no one to talk to. Kate told me she'd meet me there because she had work first thing so she just sent me the address of the spa/B&B type place and told me that the room was booked in her name.

When I finally arrived at the annoyingly out of the way but incredibly beautiful little building, surrounded by enormous oak tree's and little colourful flowers that I could never even begin to name, I parked up and grabbed my bags, slinging them over my shoulders and heading to the reception area. When I gave them Kate's name at the desk, they told me there were no reservations in that name. I tried my own name and they gave me the same answer. I was so angry. Kate was supposed to be my best friend, yet she was constantly messing me up or forgetting to tell me things when plans changed. I tried to phone her, but she didn't answer. I tried again and it only rang three times before it cut off. She was blatantly avoiding me and I just wanted to scream. And then I saw him, standing in the doorway of the B&B, a bag in hand and a serious look on his face. I groaned.

“Well, I should have known,” I mumbled moodily, realising Kate and Nick had schemed yet again.

"When will you learn that *I need time*? Why won't you let me *move on*?" I asked. The pitch of my voice increasing a tad. Nick dropped his bag and stepped forward, taking a deep breath and pinching the bridge of his nose before he spoke.

"Sasha, this isn't going to be easy for me to say, but I'm going to say it anyway. Don't walk away, please. Just listen. When the walls are closing in, and the ceiling is collapsing, you're the only person I want to talk to. Everything feels so wrong when I'm not with you and I'm so sick of it. I don't want to eat properly, and when I do, nothing tastes good. I can't read because the words always remind me of you, and when I write, I write about you, I write about us, and how badly I want us to be together, how I want to immortalise us in writing just in case you never look at me again. I want to experience that crazy, whirlwind romance that all the characters in all the books seem to have. I want to jump into the ocean with you all over again. I want to relieve our first kiss over and over until I can't breathe. I want to kiss you on a mountain top and grow old with you. I don't care if no one thinks we'll last. I don't even care if you don't think we'll last, because deep down, I know in my heart that we will go the distance and further. I know this because I love you, I am so in love with you, and I know you love me too. I know you feel this magnetism just the same as I do, pulling us towards each other with every move and breath and thought. I know you don't want to let what we have just file away in the back of our minds until the pain of not having it consumes both of our very souls. I know you feel the same as I do, I just know it, so please, if you can find it in you to give this a go, a real honest to God try, then please do. Because I am nothing without you, I'm so in love with you, and I'm sorry for that, but you're just going to have to deal with it because I can't go another day pretending I'm not."

He finally stopped talking and I felt my heart swell. I couldn't breathe because my lungs were in my throat, and I was completely blind because my eyes were filled with tears. I'd never felt such love in my life. I'd never been so overwhelmed by the pain of not being close to someone. In that moment, I realised that I couldn't fathom a life without Nick. Not right now, not at this time, and he was completely right. I did feel that magnetism, and that immense, overbearing, powerful, all-consuming love that he felt. In that moment, once I'd dried my eyes and could see that face more clearly than I ever had, I wanted to shrivel up and turn to ashes at how clouded with anger my vision had been. I dropped my bags, just as Nick had his, and threw myself into his arms, pressing my lips to his more through need than want as his strong arms wrapped around my waist. I had never felt so at home or so happy. It was like the first time we'd kissed but intensified by the hurt and anger and pain of being apart. I knew this was love. It couldn't be anything else. I'd been wrong to think I could ever have walked away from him, or gotten over him. I should have known that

I would never have felt complete if I'd have stuck to my decision to never see him again. It hurt so god damn much to think about the time we'd spent apart and it hurt me even more remembering that it had been my decision. I felt so awful. There were tears running down my cheeks as we held on to each other as if one of us would disappear if we let go. Eventually we broke apart, hearing the receptionist cough at our highly public display of affection. Nick told her his name, and just like magic, she presented him with the key to our room, with an annoying note from Kate that basically said, "I told you so."

We headed up to the room hand in hand, and when we finally got inside, we saw that the whole room was covered in rose petals. I sent a silent thank you to Kate before Nick's mouth was back on mine and we were suddenly too focused on the moment to really care about anything else. Feeling his body and lips against mine just wasn't enough anymore. We needed each other in a new way. After all of the pent up emotion finally being released, we needed to be close to each other in a way we never had been. In a way, I never had been with anyone. Before I knew it, we were in a race to be closer, have less between us. Even our clothes were a hindrance, so we decided they were probably just better off on the floor in the end. I'd always expected my first time to be nerve wracking, scary and awkward, but with Nick, it just felt right. We moulded together perfectly like we were made for each other, and as we lost ourselves in the moment, we became one. It was a whirlwind of heat, love, kisses and healing. It was pure perfection, and it felt right.

As the light faded and the moon replaced the sun as our only source of light, we stayed wrapped in each other's arms, scared to let go in case this happiness was too fleeting. We knew better than anyone that something could take away this moment in a second and we didn't want to admit that truth. I sat up, now in Nick's t-shirt and my pyjama shorts. I shifted myself, so I was facing him with legs crossed, while he sat rested against the headboard. I took the hand that he wasn't using to prop his head up and took a deep breath.

"What's up?" he asked, shifting so that he could brush my hair behind my ear.

"Okay. You told me how you feel and I know that took a lot, so it's time to tell you how I feel. My upbringing was different from yours. I didn't have the parents you do and I didn't have the same struggles, but I did have struggles. I had an ex that treated me like the scum of the earth, and I didn't really have any true friends. I was cheated on and stalked and it was really, really scary. Eventually, my parents decided we should move and we did but then I was faced with the struggles of finding new friends and making new connections. I found a great job, but I never made that special connection that I'd always craved, until I met this cute guy in this shabby bar that I was just instantly drawn to. We ended up making out on the dance floor, and sparks flew. It felt amazing, and the idea of never seeing that guy again drove me mad, so we added each other on Facebook, and we talked and spent a crazy night together, swimming in the ocean and connecting like we'd known each other forever. We got close and we fell in love, but then something came between us, and when we were driven apart, I felt like I was going to die. Everything felt wrong, and I didn't want to eat or talk or even dream. I just wanted to not exist anymore because, without him, everything felt blurry and ugly. Nick, I do feel that magnetism, and I do love you. I don't care about what Jenna has to say anymore, and I'm sorry it took me so long to figure that out. Nothing matters except the fact that we love each other. Not your job, not Jenna, not my parents, or my age, not my friends, or your friends, or your mother. Nothing should ever come between us again, and if anything or anyone tries, we just have to fight them, and we can, if we do it together. I love you Nick. I never want to spend another second thinking about how crap it is being without you. I don't want to worry about anything that concerns us because, at the end of the day, it doesn't matter if I can still be in your arms when it all comes tumbling down. Being with you feels right and nothing is going to make me forget that this time."

I felt relieved that I'd finally gotten it off my chest. Nick had already said it all and completely stolen the romantic limelight, but I didn't care, because he knew now how much I loved him, and I knew, for the first time, that someone truly loved me. Not in a way a parent loves a child or the way a friend loves another friend, but the true, heart crushingly real way as soul mates love each other. Nick grinned that devilish grin that I loved so much and leant forward to kiss me. His fingers tangled in my hair as I responded, the moment getting intense and turning into another black and white moment of pure, unfiltered passion.

I woke up just as the sun was rising. I wanted to stay quiet as I didn't wake Nick up, so I slipped out of bed as carefully as I possibly could. I stumbled over to the window where the large ledge made a perfect space for me to sit on and hoisted myself onto the windowsill. I curled my knees up to my chest and braced myself for the morning chill as I opened the window. The air was fresh and clean, bringing the smell of winter and golden leaves. I smiled to myself and closed my eyes. For the first time in a long time I was happy. I rolled my head to the side to glance at Nick and was taken aback by just how gorgeous he looked in the glow of the rising sun. His arms were folded behind his head, while his long, faintly muscular torso moved peacefully as he breathed. His long, dark lashes cast shadows over his cheekbones and his perfectly pink mouth stayed parted just slightly in the middle. He had the faintest smile on those lips, as if he was having some secret adventure in his dreams, and that thought alone made me giddy with euphoria. I lowered myself from the windowsill, closing the window so we wouldn't catch a chill and padded as quietly as I could into the bathroom. I brushed my teeth and then turned on the shower. I was expecting it to be a crappy trickle of lukewarm water, but it turned out to be better than my shower at home. The water pummelled my skin in thick droplets, massaging my muscles and scalp like it was some kind of miracle water.

It wasn't long before the stirrings of a finally waking man were to be heard in the other room. I wasn't expecting him to wander into the bathroom while I was still showering. I suddenly felt shy as I realised the shower curtain was see-through, and I was aware that my entire body was just out there for the world to see. Nick grinned as he looked me up and down, something rather animal hinting in his eyes. I rolled my own eyes and snatched my towel from the hook next to the shower, shutting off the water and covering myself before he could say anything. I stepped out and walked purposefully back to the other room, pulling on my clothes as soon as I was dry enough. I waited to hear the shower turn back on. I took the time to dry my hair, and when Nick finally emerged in nothing more than a towel, I couldn't help but grin. He still had water droplets perfectly formed on his skin while his dark hair dripped more onto his shoulders and face. He pounced without warning, tickling me until I was laughing so hard that he had to kiss me to shut me up.

"You are one beautiful woman," he whispered in my ear, sending shivers down my tingling spine. I grinned, pulling his face back to mine for another kiss.

# CHAPTER SEVENTEEN

## *Nick*

Sasha looked beautiful in the light of the rising sun. She didn't know I was awake, but as soon as she'd gotten out of bed, I felt it. I felt how empty the bed was without her by my side, and it woke me up. I watched her through half closed eyes, the light creating a halo around her body, and the slight breeze from the open window made her hair flutter out behind her in the smallest way. She was smiling to herself, looking like an angel and clearly, finally happy, just like I was. She turned her head to the side so I stayed as still as I possibly could so she wouldn't know I'd just been gawking at her while she sat there. She hopped off the windowsill and I kind of thought I was busted, until she headed to the bathroom to shower.

I laid in bed until I couldn't anymore. I barged into the bathroom and saw the most beautiful creature being showered with steaming hot water. I'd be lying if I said some pretty dirty thoughts didn't cross my mind, but I tried to keep myself in check. Sasha rolled her eyes at me and snatched her towel around her goddess body in a ninja move. I took my time showering, hoping I'd drive her as crazy as she drove me, and then wrapped one of the fluffy white towels around my waist in another attempt to drive her insane.

We ended up spending most of the morning messing around and talking. We couldn't stop touching each other: holding hands, brushing arms, cuddling or anything that would remind us that this was real and that we were back together. We didn't talk about what would happen when we got back to town, and we didn't worry. We had today to be together without complications, we would face everything else tomorrow.

By the time we left, it was already dark and we didn't want to part ways and head to our own cars. However, Sasha was due back at college for her last few days, and I needed to assess the damage in my classroom. We made plans to meet up after our days were over and vowed to text each other as soon as we were home.

*

I was dreading looking at my classroom but when I got there, it wasn't as bad as I'd imagined. I guess maybe I was wearing rose-tinted glasses because I was so happy about the weekend, but nothing seemed as bad as I thought it would be. My bookshelf was pretty much intact, bar a few scuffs and chips, but all the books were badly damaged. It made me sad to see the memories that had been held in the pages just strewn across the room, but the books were just material: they could be replaced. My desk was scratched, the locks on all of the draws were busted and all my pens and notebooks were gone. My chair was completely destroyed, and there was glass all over the floor. Okay, maybe it was pretty bad. I sat on a plastic chair and started to fill out the forms I'd been given regarding what had been damaged and what was missing. Sadly, insurance can't protect memories, and that was mostly what was missing in this room.

CJ found me about an hour after I'd finished the paperwork, clutching his own forms in one hand and a smashed picture frame in the other. I chuckled to myself when I saw that the picture inside was of him and Cat.

"You have to get over her, man," I laughed, causing him to pick up a completely mutilated book and throw it straight at my head.

"You're happy. I take it things between you and your lady are sorted now?"

"We're back together, but the issues are just as real as they were when we broke up. We just have to find a way to deal with them," I sighed, picking up my papers and following CJ out of the room to hand them in.

"Well, if you need anyone to step in with Jenna, just let me know." I nodded gratefully and told him I'd be okay, but I'd let him know if I did, and then I sighed audibly when I saw where our replacement classes were being held.

"This is going to be forty times less fun than we thought it would be." I handed CJ the piece of paper that said we would be teaching at the South College until our rooms were fixed.

He laughed, "Guess your problems just got worse again."

I punched his shoulder and followed him to the car park.

The South College did not make me happy. My classroom was basically a cupboard and only three of my students even bothered turning up. So there really was no point in even being there. Then to make matters worse, I ended up seeing Sasha while I was wandering around looking for somewhere to sit with my lunch. She was with Kate, who was whispering like the gossip she was and probably grilling Sasha over what had happened at the weekend.

We couldn't hug, wave or even smile at each other in fear of Jenna lurking somewhere. I couldn't believe we were back to having to keep things secret, at least until Sasha left the college for good at the end of the week. I guess a week wasn't even that long, but in the scheme of things, it felt like it. She text me just as I sat down, saying she was waving silently at me, which made me smile to myself. I text back saying I was waving too, and then I put my phone away because I was getting incredibly paranoid in the current situation.

It didn't take long for Jenna to seek me out. Part of me even thought that she might have been the one to trash the classrooms, but I knew deep down she wouldn't risk her own job for that. I told Jenna I couldn't talk while I was teaching, but that didn't deter her. She told me she'd come back later, and that she had to talk to me about something urgent.

I was nervous for Jenna to return. I didn't want anything to do with her so being in a tiny room with her venomous ways wasn't exactly making me jump for joy. Sasha managed to slip in to see me before she left, per request and told me that if Jenna started to make trouble, I should just leave straight away and report her for harassment or something. I laughed a lot at that and handed her my keys so that she could get into the flat if Cat wasn't home. She gave me a quick peck on the cheek and left before anyone saw her. I was starting to think she really was a ninja with how fast she was becoming.

Jenna slipped into my cupboard classroom wearing a long coat and holding a wet umbrella. "Raining?" I asked coldly, hating the edge on my voice.

"Yes. A lot actually." She threw the umbrella down onto a desk and then sat on the edge of an entirely different one.
"What did you want?" I asked.

“Well, I wanted to warn you, that if you're still with Sasha, I will catch you, and you will end up in a lot of trouble. I wanted to give you a heads up just in case you were thinking of messing your life up further.”

“Nice. Well, for your information, your little letter stunt broke us up for good, so unfortunately, you won't be able to 'catch us' because there's nothing to catch.” The lie came to my lips as easily as a Romeo and Juliet quote. It was instinct now, to protect mine and Sasha's relationship as fiercely as possible.

“Well, in that case, I have a proposal for you, Nicholas. How about, we give things another go, take it slowly, go for a drink maybe?” she asked, sickly sweet.

I laughed. “Just because you ruined my love life, does not mean I’m desperate enough to have you back in it. No, I don't want to have a drink with you, and hopefully, come Friday, I won't have to have anything to do with you ever again.”

“Well, if that's how you want it, then suit yourself. But if I catch wind of you and that tramp even being in the same room, I will make your life an absolute misery. You know I can do it. I don’t have to remind you how easily I can make things look scandalous. I have to say, the letter was genius. If I catch you together again, I might have to hurt someone."

"Fine Jenna. Just leave."

And she did.

Sasha had cooked couscous when I got home. It was delicious and she had made up the kitchen table to be really romantic, which was sweet. I didn't want to bother her with Jenna's threats yet again, but I felt like I might have to, in fear of her finding out later. I didn't bring it up until we were done with dinner and laid out on the sofa with a blanket and the TV on low while we pretty much just made out. I sat up a little and Sasha frowned.

"What?" she asked, knowing me all too well by now.

"Jenna still wants to ruin us," I admitted, making Sasha sigh and sit up fully.

"Well, Jenna can suck my dick," Sasha growled.

"Attractive," I remarked, making her smirk a little and admit she was being childish.

"I don't see what's left to do now, aside from just letting her do her worst," she sighed, putting her head in her hands.

"Yeah, look how far that got us last time though. I have no idea what to do about her to be honest," I admitted.

We went to bed at around one in the morning after far too long trying to find a way of getting rid of Jenna that didn't involve murder. Sasha had some worryingly good murder plans if it came to it, but I did have to remind her that murder was in fact illegal. She fell asleep soon after that, and I laid awake with her in my arms, making the decision to just confront Jenna once and for all, whether she threw my life into turmoil or not. It was time to stop living in fear of the woman, but I'd have to wait until Friday, when Sasha was finally free to go.

*

Friday came around all too slowly, but it did come around. I wasn't exactly looking forward to telling Jenna to shove it, but I was so sick of everything she'd done that I just wanted this ridiculous feud to end.

She was in her classroom when I finally found her. I knew this was the place Sasha had slapped her, and the thought of how that must've looked did make me smirk, as wrong as that is.

She smiled at me, "What brings you here? Rethinking my offer?" she asked, making me shake my head.

"No Jenna. But I do need to talk to you, despite how depressing that thought is."

"Ouch. Go ahead."

"The truth is Jen, I need to come clean about something. Me and Sasha? We are back together, and we're staying together, regardless of what you think or what you want or what you do, and we're staying that way. Get me sacked, fine. Get me banished from the country, whatever. Do what you like, but you need to know that *we are done*, and Sasha and I are together. I don't care what you do anymore, I really, truly don't, because I love her, and I actually want to spend my life with her, so you might as well just give up." I let out a breath and watched Jenna's face basically melt. She put a hand to her forehead and I actually began to think she was realising the errors of her ways until she opened her mouth.

"Well, I guess I'll have to contact the police, won't I? They'll be very interested in hearing about your relationship with a student."

"But Jenna, she isn't, wasn't and will never be my student. I don't even work for this college. You have absolutely no case. But you, on the other hand, you harassed a student, sent a fake letter to her parents, intentionally messed up her essay and provoked her. Now that seems a little more worth an investigation to me. How about you? How does that sound to you?"

I don't know where it came from. It had never even occurred to me to look at it from that angle until last night, but watching her resolve completely crumble made me feel triumphant like I'd won. Sure, I could never have taken this angle if she hadn't pursued her attack on Sasha and completely messed us up for a few weeks, but I could use it now, and I knew it was working. Jenna couldn't lose her job, because if she did, her parents would be disappointed, and if her parents were disappointed, they'd cut off her ridiculously high allowance that she still received at 26. No wonder she still acted like a teenager with her nose out of joint. She was still being treated like one. I'm pretty sure these thoughts crossed her mind as she considered what I'd just said, as she fought to think up an argument, but of course, she didn't have one, because she had been in the wrong. She should never have treated Sasha the way she did, regardless of her relationship with me, and she was finally realising it. I then showed her the phone I'd been using to record our conversation.

"Shit!" she exclaimed. "Shit, shit, shit, shit, shit. What have I done?" she asked with tears in her eyes. I felt sorry for her, but I didn't want to fall for it, so I just sighed, turning to leave.

"You've got a chance to make it right now Jenna, so take it. If you don't, I've got everything I need to get you into a lot of trouble." And then I walked away.

I was pretty sure I'd won, so I phoned Sasha and asked her if she'd come over. She told me she'd be at the flat soon, so I just made my own way back and waited for her to arrive.

She was in her pyjamas when she got to mine, which actually just consisted of some shorts and one of my sweatshirts.

"Hi," she breathed, kissing me quickly before pushing past me into the flat. She poked her head into the living room to say hello to Cat and then went through to the kitchen and made herself a glass of water.

"Make yourself at home," I joked, watching a grin slide on to her face.

I loved that grin. It was the thing I looked forward to most when I knew I was going to see Sasha. When she smiled, it was like everything would be fine no matter what happened because if Sasha was smiling, the world was smiling.

"So, what did you want to talk to me about?" she asked, biting into a strawberry she'd just retrieved from the fridge.

"I spoke to Jenna today and I think we finally won," I grinned, waiting for her celebration. It took her a moment but she finally laughed with a hint of relief in her tone.

"Well, that's amazing Nick!" she squealed, jumping up to sit on my lap and kiss me before adding a "but."

"But, there may be another struggle on our hands now." She hung her head a little and mumbled into my shoulder. "My parents want to have dinner with you, and Cat and CJ and uh, Kate, so that they can fully understand everything that went on." She kissed my neck to distract me but there wasn't much room in my currently exploding brain for distraction.

"What?"

# CHAPTER EIGHTEEN
*Sasha*

Nick was not excited to meet my parents again. After the whole letter fiasco he was convinced they would try to separate us again, but he didn't know them like I did. He'd only experienced the one time they'd ever acted that way. He asked me what he should wear and glared hilariously when I told him 'whatever you want' causing me to pick out his nicest black jeans and a grey button down shirt that looked incredibly sexy on him. He smiled gratefully and kissed my forehead before telling me to get lost. I laughed and grabbed my bag so I could head home and get ready myself. Cat and Kate were highly excited about the event, thinking it would create great gossip if anything went down. CJ had been texting Nick non-stop since he found out he was required, to ask why exactly he was required.

*

I was pretty surprised when my parents asked me to invite Nick and our friends over for dinner. I wasn't quite sure if it was a peace making gesture or a way for them to grill him. The only way to find out was to make the dinner date happen. They asked me about it in the weirdest way. I was walking down the stairs to make myself a snack and my dad called me into the living room. I grabbed my food first, walking into the other room with a slice of peanut butter on toast in one hand and a pint of diet coke in the other.

"What's up?" I asked, freaking a little when he asked me to sit down.

I was starting to wonder if something had happened or if they were going to tell me they wanted to move or something, but once I'd sat, his face brightened a little and my mum was grinning.

"Sasha, we'd like to host a meal for you and your friends, to get to know them," she stated.

"Okay, why?" I bit, feeling like there was some kind of catch.

"Well, we didn't give Nick a fair chance, as you've let us know a few times now, and we feel like we're not really in touch with your life at the moment. You've got new people in your life, and we'd like to meet them, talk to them, and see for ourselves the greatness you see in them. Of course you can invite Kate too, seeing as you're still as inseparable as when you first met, but we'd like to meet these other people you talk about, Cat and CJ, is it? They seem to have been included in a lot of your stories recently, so we'd like to find out more about them. How does next Saturday sound?"

The spiel took me a moment to take in and I had to give her credit for not even giving me a choice, but at least she was trying to understand the change in my life.

“Next Saturday should be good. I'll have to check with the others though. Obviously they might have plans,” I said nervously.

“Well, if they can't make it, we'll reschedule,” my dad said, smiling.

I was defeated. There was absolutely no way any of us were getting out of this. “Okay then,” I smiled, probably a little wide eyed.

I grabbed my drink and a now cold slice of toast and headed back upstairs, only to get a call from Nick asking if I'd pop to his. I didn't bother changing, there was no point when I'd only end up staying there anyway. So I grabbed a bag, told my parents I was going to see Kate, just to save having the awkward talks about staying with your boyfriend, and then I left.

*

I'd made the decision to stay at Nick's the Friday before the meal because that way, I could prepare both him and Cat for what could potentially come. I told my parents I was staying at Kate's again. When I got home from Nick's, I thought I was busted. Kate was sitting in my living room with my parents and chatting animatedly with them while they nodded and smiled.

"Hey," I called, trying to play it cool before the 'rents began to scream at me, but they never did, because Kate, being the hero she was, saved the day.

"How on earth did I get here before you if we left at the same time?" she asked, winking when my parents weren't looking.

"Oh, I just went to town to get some money out, considering the one by the shops isn't working. I just thought it was a good idea, we always end up needing stuff last minute for these meals." I looked pointedly at my mother, who grinned sheepishly, probably remembering the countless times she'd planned a big meal and then sent me out three or four times to get the stuff she'd forgotten.

I was so incredibly lucky that Kate had thought on her feet. I told everyone we were going to head upstairs and waited for Kate to get up off her arse to follow me before actually leading the way.

Kate catapulted herself onto my bed, completely messing up my pillows as she did so, before leaning over the edge to retrieve an old magazine from under my bed to read while I had my shower.

"You're way too at home here," I bit, grabbing my towels from my radiator and heading straight to my bathroom.

"You wouldn't have me any other way!" she shouted aggressively.

Halfway through my shower, I heard my computer turn on. Kate was bored already, so I knew I'd have to hurry up before she broke something just for fun. I stepped out of the shower and wrapped my hair in a towel, drying off with the other and throwing on a large promotional t-shirt I'd gotten from Fivers a while ago with my pyjama shorts. I flicked on the switch next to the mirror to turn on the de-steamer and then went to tell Kate she could get in the shower. She grumbled some comments about how she didn't understand why I always took hours in there but didn't respond when I asked her to speak up.

I threw open the doors to my wardrobe and sighed. I had absolutely no idea what to wear. I grumbled to myself and made weird aggravated noises until I finally decided on three potential outfits. The dress code was smart casual, so I didn't want to look too dressy, but at the same time, it was always fun to dress up. Laid out on my bed was a shortish, red, strapless dress with a puffy skirt and a few silver rhinestones. A black, three quarter length sleeved dress with a white lace skirt, and a sparkly, grey, backless, spaghetti strap dress that looked killer with silver sparkly stilettos was next to it. I paced back and forth, sighing and mumbling as I tried to decide which was the most suitable. It became evident that I was never going to be able to figure it out on my own, so I began to get my hair and makeup done in an effort to calm my slowly appearing nerves. I dried my hair and then straightened it before I began the painful process of curling, spraying and pinning it to achieve perfect ringlets, instead of the wavy wildness I usually got when I left it to dry on its own. I then rubbed moisturiser into my hands and massaged my face, applying a translucent power to eliminate the shine. I then worked on creating a neutral eye with thick, feline eyeliner and dark red lips.

Kate finally got out of the shower and wolf whistled at me. I rolled my eyes, asking her to help me decide on a dress before she sorted her hair out. Her eyes took in each dress thoroughly before she picked up the grey one.

“Definitely this one. I remember when you wore it to Gina's birthday that time and drove that waiter mental. I remember being jealous of how great you looked, so definitely that one.”

I was flattered by her comments. Kate was never jealous of anyone, she had no reason to be. However, even her saying she thought I looked that good in the grey dress was enough to convince me to throw it on before I could go back to being indecisive.

“What are you wearing?” I asked when she finally finished drying her hair.

She didn't need to do anything else with it then, it fell glossily to just below her waist and looked like it was been styled by a professional without any effort what so ever. She pulled a tight black dress out of her overnight bag but then put it back.

"I was going to wear that, but I actually really like that red one." She grinned at me, in her own little way of asking to borrow the dress without actually asking, and I nodded.

"Fine, just don't get it ruined okay?" I laughed, flopping into my computer chair to check my emails and social networks. I had a Facebook message from Nick that was just a picture of him and CJ, dressed as smartly as they could be without wearing full on suits. They were both holding a bottle of beer each and looking like they were about to crap their pants. I laughed a little too loudly and double clicked on the picture to show Kate. She laughed too and then asked me to find out what Cat was wearing. Cat told Nick we'd just have to wait and see, but she promised it was suitable for parents. I'll admit that.

When everyone arrived, I was so incredibly nervous that my hands were shaking. Nick took them in his own and told me to calm down, before releasing my hand to wrap an arm around my shoulders. I instantly felt calmer, happier and less nervous. It still struck me as crazy how one simple gesture from the right person could change how you felt in a second. I leant into Nick for a second before pulling away to lead everyone into the living room. I introduced everyone one by one and then offered them all a drink and a seat. Kate and Cat offered to help me get them while my parents started to chat with CJ and Nick. Cat was wearing a peach coloured silk dress with a netted skirt. She looked like the model she was and I was completely jealous of her perfect-for-makeup face. I grabbed three beers from the fridge, poured three glasses of some random wine I couldn't pronounce the name of for Cat, Kate and my mum, then poured a pint of diet coke for myself.

"So, you ready?" Cat asked, already excited for whatever was about to go down. I shook my head and lead the way back to the living room, choosing to sit between Nick and CJ on the sofa instead of unintentionally splitting the room into men and women.

The evening actually started smoothly. Nothing was really said that could trigger any kind of argument and I was starting to relax, until my mother sent us all to the table for starters. My mother managed to put her foot right in her mouth by mentioning Jenna right off the bat.

"So, Nick, crazy ex you have there," she laughed, thinking she was being funny.

I choked on a mouthful of coke, while everyone else went dead silent.

"Uh, yeah. I didn't know she was crazy when I met her," he replied with a hint of annoyance in his voice which caused CJ to jump in.

"Jenna was actually my friend before she was Nick's girlfriend. I introduced them when we started going to Uni together and almost forced them to go on their first date. None of us knew what was lurking in the recesses of her brain," he laughed, trying to lighten the mood.

"What made you realise she was cracked?" My dad asked, looking from CJ to Nick questioningly.

"Actually, we only really found out when she started laying into Nick and Sash," Cat said sharply.

I dropped my head into my hands and groaned. "How about we just don't talk about this," I sighed, needing this conversation to move on.

"Well, it's only right we know more about Nick's past. He's going out with you and we all know you don't exactly have a good track record when it comes to men," my mother snapped.

"Whatever. You don't need to know about Jenna because she's done messing, okay." Nick squeezed my knee under the table to try to calm me down. I smiled gratefully in his direction.

"Okay, subject change!" Kate shouted. "Cat's a model. You may have seen her on TV and in magazines a few times," she said to my mother, who then squinted at Cat for what seemed like hours.

"Actually, I thought you looked familiar! What made you get into modelling then?" she asked.

"Well, I wanted to get away and do something different, and I just so happened to be lucky enough to get 'discovered' I guess. I've been working in the industry ever since. Makeup artists like my facial structure, some photographers have a problem with my weight, but they can stuff it. I've been threatened with sacking a gazillion times for refusing to drop any smaller than and eight but my agent actually supports me which is rare. I've been taking a break recently. A stalker has basically forced me into moving in with my brother until they find him, but I'll get back out there as soon as he's found. I was supposed to do a fashion show in London a couple of weeks ago but the risk of him finding me wasn't something my agent wanted to chance," she smiled, taking a sip of her wine before she saw my mum's face drop.

"So you've both been involved with crazies then? How about your parents, have they ever had anything like this happen to them?" she asked, a little anger colouring her tone.

I stood up then, not wanting either of them to have to go through the pain of talking about their mother. "If you remember, mother, I had a stalker too. I made bad decisions too, and you didn't exactly hate Jase before we broke up. So, don't judge them because if you're going down that road, you need to look to yourselves too. You've got more skeletons in your wardrobe than your average serial killer so just *stop!*" I ended up shouting the last word, too angry to cope with all the hypocrisy anymore, and then I left the table.

I sat on my bed and breathed deeply, with my body hunched over to try and get rid of the queasy feeling that was gripping me. Eventually, Nick found me but I was pretty sure that my parents had seen sense and sent him. He closed my door behind him and sat beside me on my bed, rubbing large circles into my back soothingly.

"Hey," he said softly.

"Hey back."

"So, that was eventful," he remarked, making me snort a little.

"I'm so sorry. They're never, ever like this usually. I don't know what's wrong with them."

"It's okay. Cat thinks it's funny and you know I wasn't exactly expecting them to be making best friends with me," he laughed, pulling me back so we were both laying down. I turned on my side to cuddle up to him.

"I'm still sorry. Anyway, I should probably stop acting like a five year old and get back to the party," I sighed, kissing Nick playfully before pulling him up. "Come on. You can check out my room properly some other time," I winked, dragging him out with me.

The rest of the night was rocky. Everyone was polite to one another, but there was definite tension in the air. Arguments brewed but never quite came to a head and nobody wanted to say anything that was going to set me off again. I did catch CJ smirking at me a few times, probably re-living my outburst, but at least he had the sense not to say anything.

Once everyone had left, Kate and I sat dissecting the night in the living room while my parents went off to bed, hopefully hanging their heads in shame. Kate told me that Nick had really stepped up when I'd walked off, but she wouldn't tell me anymore. I fell asleep wondering if my parents would ever just take a moment to accept Nick into their lives because forever would be a long time for them to hold a grudge.

# CHAPTER NINETEEN
*Nick*

Sasha's parents' meal was a total disaster. It was clear they didn't approve of me. When they started on Cat, I wondered if it was more that they didn't approve of Sasha having a secret life for the past couple of months than the people she'd spent that life with. I wasn't sure I'd find out soon.

When Sasha stormed off, I felt it was time to speak my mind. She always told me how amazing her parents were, but tonight they were acting like children. They were upsetting their daughter who they knew had been through a hell of a lot. Her mother stood up to follow her, but I stopped her.

"Sasha always tells me how amazing you are. She goes on and on about how much she loves you to the moon and back and how you've always done anyt and everything to keep her safe. But let me ask you this, where were you when Jenna was threatening her? Where were you when she told you point blank that the letter was a lie? Where were you when she was so down over everything that had happened, that she drank herself silly and ended up staying out until she was sober enough to come home?" Her parents both gasped in shock, hearing about that last one for the first time. "Yeah. Your daughter that doesn't drink, she was so pissed she couldn't even stand up straight, and you didn't even know about it. So before you judge me or my family, take a moment to look at how you've been treating your own." I spun around and began to head towards the stairs, Kate called after me, telling me which door was Sasha's.

After Sasha and I got back downstairs, the evening continued in what felt like a bubble of awkwardness, and we were all relieved when it was time to leave.

CJ stayed at ours, sleeping in the living room with Cat, even though I didn't exactly approve. The next morning, I got a phone call from Sasha's father on their home line, asking me to meet him by the restaurant by the sea wall restaurant in town. I got dressed quickly and made my way there, thinking this would make for an interesting conversation.

Sasha's father was sitting on the sea wall with a cup of coffee in his hands. He didn't have one for me, but I decided not to make trouble for myself. "What's up?" I asked, sitting beside him awkwardly.

"This isn't going to be easy for me to say, but I wanted to apologise for mine and my wife's behaviour. Not just last night, but over the past couple of weeks. I don't know how much you know about Sasha's past, but we're very protective of her, and we have let that cloud our judgement recently. I can see that you're a good person, no matter what has happened in your own past. The way you stood up to protect Sasha last night, especially against us, made me realise that you just want to keep her safe and happy as much as we do. That being said, I'd like to invite you over for a more casual visit, maybe once the wounds of last night are healed and forgotten, so that we can get to know you without judgements and without arguments. It's evident that Sasha plans to be with you for a very long time, and once she has her heart set on something, it's not easy to change her mind. So, yes, I'd like to apologise, and make a plan to make amends." He held out his hand for me to shake in a gesture of kindness and I took it.

"I'd like that. I didn't want to be rude to you or your wife last night, but I don't think she made it clear to you quite how much she's been through recently. And she's pretty protective over me and my sister anyway, so I guess there were more reasons than one for all the outbursts," I smiled, taking my apology as far as it could go without completely kissing Mr. Santiago's ass.

We talked for a little while about my intentions towards his daughter, and eventually parted ways. I grabbed myself a coffee before making my way back to my car and texted Sasha to ask if she'd like to come to a make-up meal at the flat.

The meal consisted of couscous, salad and for CJ, Cat, Kate and myself, alcohol. We spent the whole of the meal laughing over the fiasco that was the night before, and when we were full and drowsy, we all went to the living room to watch some films. Sasha and I curled up on our usual sofa, wrapped in each other's arms and a blanket with a bowl of salted popcorn between us. Kate sat on the floor in front of us with an entire bowl of sweet popcorn to herself. Much to my surprise, Cat and CJ sat together on the armchair, completely oblivious to the three of us staring at them while they outright canoodled. I coughed, causing Sasha to slap my chest.

"Leave them," she whispered, "It's sweet," she smiled, turning back to the tv and averting her eyes.

"Sweet?!" I whispered back, "It's disgusting! He's supposed to be my best friend and he's eating my sister's face!"

Sasha laughed at me and moved so that she could kiss me. "They're happy, we're happy, Kate's happy as long as Leo DiCaprio is on screen, so let's just leave them to it. Happy is good, Nick, we all deserve it," she smiled, reaching up to scratch the side of my head.

She was right, we were all happy, and that was all that mattered. After everything that had gone on in a matter of weeks, it was right that we took a moment to enjoy it, instead of turning it into more drama that we didn't need. I kissed the top of her head and settled down properly to watch the film with a smile on my face. I would never admit it to her, but Sasha was a lot smarter than most people. She lived life exactly how she wanted to, she followed her impulses, took risks and let things go when they didn't need to be addressed. She held people together and she didn't even realise it. They say home is where the heart is, but I was almost certain that was wrong because it seemed to me, that at least for the people who knew her, home was wherever Sasha was.

When we eventually made it to bed that night, Sash was already half asleep. I got into bed beside her and slipped my arm over her waist. “I love you millions, wonderful lady,” I whispered in her ear.

“I love you too.”

“How did I get so lucky?” I asked, breathing her in.

“I think they call it Kismet,” she replied, a smile creeping onto her lips as she drifted into a dream world.

THE END...

# COMING SOON

## The Intern

# THANK YOU

I'd like to say a huge thank you to *you.* Yes, you; for reading Kismet and joining Nick and Sasha's world for a moment in time. I hope you loved the gang just as much as I do. Thank you all so much for everything you've done to help me spread the word about Kismet, for leaving your reviews and thoughts and for letting me share this book with you.

Keep an eye out for my next release, check out some of my poetry or fawn over pictures of my pets with me over at:

www.instagram.com/MissAlieWrites
www.facebook.com/AlieDayAuthor
www.twitter.com/MissAlieWrites
Goodreads: Alie Day

A publication by Tamarind Hill Press
www.tamarindhillpress.co.uk

**TAMARiND HiLL**
**.PRESS**

Lightning Source UK Ltd.
Milton Keynes UK
UKHW040631051219
354823UK00001B/164/P